YARDING
BRAXTON

STELLA WILLIAMS

SERPENTINE CREATIVE LLC

Editing

Line Edits by Ali Williams

www.aliwilliams.org

CONTENTS

Content Warnings

This book contains themes related to Domestic Abuse, Post Traumatic Stress, Grief, and Mental Health Issues.

YARDING

/ yärd/
  verb
- 1.store or transport (timber) in or to a log yard

"he is the last logger to be using a sled for yarding logs"

Source: Oxford Dictionary

CHAPTER 1

Carmen Quinn held her head high as she strode through the lobby of the Mulberry Corinthian and straight to the first-floor lounge—her red fedora pulled down to partially shield her face, matching trench coat swishing around her thigh-high leather boots. She ignored the stares. Yes, she was dressed as Carmen San Diego. And yes, she was aware that Halloween wasn't for another month. Who cared? She took a seat at the bar and ordered a glass of the house red.

The Corinthian was truly a luxury establishment. One she could barely afford, even with all the extra gigs Imena had helped her secure through Sowell Sisters Events and Boutique. She'd only paid for one night, fully expecting to spend the weekend in Noah's much more expensive room at K Hotel. But now she would have to change her flight or, at the very least, her choice of hotel. Whichever was the cheapest option now that she would also be looking for a new place to stay once she got back to Sowell City.

She took a sip and let it warm her throat and body. Coming here had been a mistake. She'd known it would be, but she hadn't been able to help herself. Some sick part of her had wanted the confirmation that she and Noah were done for good this time. If she were being honest, they had been over before she moved in with him, but she hadn't been ready to let go. Now there was nowhere for her to hide.

Ten years of back and forth, of her being his little secret in high school, then finally out in the open through college. Two years more of playing the fool, following him to Sowell City. Had she really thought dressing up as the character he had a fetish for would rekindle the spark between them? It hadn't mattered. She'd gone up to his room at K Hotel, all ready to surprise him on his supposed business trip, only to find another woman there. The perky blonde answered the door in the blue shirt she'd bought him for Christmas last year.

Carmen should have made a fucking scene. Should have barged in there and let him have it, but instead, she claimed to have the wrong room and rushed back to the elevators and straight to her hotel across town. If she'd been any less of a mess, she'd have probably gone straight to her room, grabbed her shit and got the hell out of dodge. The problem? Her limited bank account and sudden need of new living arrangements. So instead, she'd found herself heading to the bar to drown her sorrows and come up with a plan.

She finished her first glass of red and signaled for another, wishing for the first time that she had a taste for the harder stuff, but wine was all she could handle. She had already downed her first cup a little too quickly. She could feel the familiar tingly feeling she got when she was approaching her limit. She would definitely have to take her time with this second glass.

What would your parents think of you now?

Carmen shook that thought away. Mulberry was only an hour from Belbridge, the small town where she'd grown up; where her parents still currently lived and the church her father ran thrived. If she were desperate enough, she could just go there. What would her parents say if she showed up on their doorstep? A whole lot of judgmental bullshit along the lines of why buy the cow when she gave the milk for free. Then her mother would begin her ranting about how she should never have named her Carmen. That her fate had been all but sealed by that one decision.

She took another gulp of wine despite telling herself she was going to take things slow. There was no way in hell she would end up on their doorstep. She wasn't that desperate. Of course, part of her still wished for her parents' approval, and missed the love and support they'd shown her before she became a vessel of sin in her parents' eyes. If only that approval didn't come with locking away everything she'd come to actually like about herself.

The best choice, her only choice, was to go back to Sowell City and finally learn to be her own person. Carmen was only just beginning to realize who she was, after so many years catering to her parents and then catering to Noah's whims. It was time for her to stop living for others and start living for herself. She took a small faux sip of her wine and pulled out her phone, flipping through her friends' social media photos.

Her friends, her sweet amazing friends that she had finally allowed herself to have after years of letting Noah ruin all chances of a social life outside of him. The friends who'd encouraged her passion for photography and helped her get her studio off the ground. Her found family.

She scowled; she could have been out hiking this weekend. She could have been adding more work to her portfolio, but instead, she followed her cheating ass boyfriend to Mulberry. Amayah and Scarlett were not going to believe this bullshit. Well, maybe they would. Now that Carmen knew the truth about Noah, her friends' subtle hints and warnings took on new meaning. Then there was Imena with her cryptic text about fateful encounters on this trip. Not quite a warning, but damn if she hadn't been correct about that shit.

Carmen was so caught up in her thoughts she barely noticed the man taking the empty seat next to her. The only thing she did notice was a change in the tingling inebriation she felt. Her body shifting from loose and relaxed to flushed with awareness. She looked up from her phone. Just a casual glance at the mountain of a man who'd chosen the seat directly next to her. She glanced around at the plethora of chairs; there were plenty more for him to grab. He was so wide, he made the barstool look like baby bear's from the three bears, and she wondered if it would last under his weight.

He wore a suit but no tie. The collar of his crisp white button-down opened a few buttons, revealing a generous tuft of golden-brown chest hair just a shade or two darker than the skin peeking underneath. Carmen hadn't realized she'd been staring or how long she'd been staring until a thick, calloused finger caught her chin and tilted it up until she was looking at the man's face instead of his chest.

"My eyes are up here, Ms. San Diego," He chuckled.

She bit her lip as she took in his features; high cheekbones, a square jaw that was already showing signs of thick stubble growing in, and a crooked nose. When she finally turned her gaze up to his, she gasped, hazel eyes glinting with amusement at her blatant perusal. She tore her gaze away and took a gulp of her wine that should have been just a sip. Thankfully, the bartender came over to take the man's drink order.

"What will you be having, sir?" The bartender asked.

The man didn't take his gaze off of her. Carmen felt it all over. The heat grew inside of her and melded with the warmth of the alcohol in her belly before shooting straight to her core. She clenched her legs together in a failed attempt to stifle the arousal gathering between her legs.

"If you need suggestions-" the bartender began, but instead of ordering a drink, the man slid a fifty-dollar bill across the bar. "For the lady's drinks."

Carmen's eyes flew up to his, ready to tell him she could pay for her own drinks but the words didn't come. The feel of his thick callused fingers sliding something into her hand dried up whatever she was about to say.

"If you want to indulge whatever little fantasy was going through your head right now, I'll be in penthouse suite 102. If not, just drop the key at the front desk," he said, before getting up and walking out.

Carmen followed his movements, eyes wide with shock and disbelief. He had the swagger of a man who knew what he had to offer, in bed and out. She bit her lip and looked down at the key card in her hand. Her heart raced with adrenaline caused by equal parts excitement and outrage.

Did he really just hand me his room key? Who picks up women at a hotel bar? Should I...

Carmen wasn't going to finish that thought. Of course, he'd propositioned her. She was a woman alone dressed like a fictional character at a luxury hotel. What was more surprising was that someone else hadn't approached her sooner. Carmen decided not to take it as a slight. She should clearly take it as a compliment. She pulled out her phone to text her friends.

Group Text Imena, Amayah, Scarlett
C: I just got propositioned in a hotel bar.
A: What are you doing in a hotel bar? Where's Noah?
S: Is the guy hot, and yeah, what happened with Noah?
C: Noah's not my problem anymore. The guy was super-hot. He paid for my drinks and slid me his room key.
I: Climb that mountain

Carmen shook her head at Imena's reply. Imena's intuition was the stuff of legend around Sowell City, so Carmen wasn't entirely shocked that she somehow knew the man in question was definitely a mountain.

S: Normally, I'm all for a casual hook-up, but I'm worried. I want to know what happened with Noah.
A: Me too. When is your flight back again?

C: He's not MY problem anymore. I'm done with all things Noah, especially tonight. My flight leaves Sunday, but I might move it up

A: That Bastard!

S: So when's the castration party happening?

C: It's not? I'm angrier with myself right now.

I: Again, my vote is to climb the mountain. The earliest flight won't be until later tomorrow anyway.

S: Imena's right. If you want to revenge fuck some hotel hottie and deal with your Noah feelings later, I can't say I wouldn't do the same.

A: Do you want me to call Sinai? She's really good at pretending to be me, you know, in case you need the extra support tonight.

Carmen sighed. She appreciated her friend's offer but she wouldn't be taking her up on it. The last thing she needed was for her friend to call her super twin over to console her.

C: Thanks for the worry, guys, but I think I'll just retire to my own room tonight.

S: With or without the hotel hottie?

I: Definitely with the Mountain.

A: Ignore them, get some rest.

Carmen tucked her phone away and picked up the hotel key card. It felt heavier than when the man first handed it to her. Like a token of the fates. The smart thing to do, the responsible thing to do, would be to turn the card in at the front desk. There was no guarantee that the man would be good in bed or that, even if he was, it would make her feel any differently about herself or her current situation. That was a lot to ask from a one-night stand anyway. Carmen left the second glass of red wine on the bar and headed toward the front desk. She would drop the key off, say she found it on the floor before heading to the row of elevators.

"Checking out?" The front desk clerk asked as Carmen handed over the key.

"No, I found it on the floor over there," Carmen said pointing at nothing but in the general direction of the entrance.

The clerk smirked as if she knew Carmen was lying. The entrance was the opposite direction she had come from. "Thank you for turning it in. Is there anything else I can help you with?"

"Um, no. Thank you," Carmen said and turned away from the desk.

Carmen would love to say she wasn't second-guessing herself as she walked toward the alcove where the elevators were. Even knowing she'd made the right decision, part of her couldn't help but wonder how the heat exchanged between her and the stranger would translate in the bedroom. Maybe she would use the stranger as fantasy fodder to pleasure herself, before calling it a night.

The alcove was mostly empty, a group of women, giggling about the night's previous adventures, stood in front of the bank of elevators. It was only as she got closer that she realized they were giggling for reasons other than having a good time. Carmen cringed upon seeing the man who had thrown her for a loop leaning against the wall, waiting to go up. She made a point not to openly gawk at him, tipping her hat lower over her eyes and staring at the ground to avoid eye contact.

The elevator opened and for a moment, Carmen hesitated. Maybe she should wait for the next one, but what if he waited for the next one too? She rushed forward, pressing herself into the far corner of the elevator, hoping that the group of women heading up to their own room would be enough of a buffer when they all crowded in.

Braxton should have just gone up to his suite and called it a night. His brother's wedding had been fun until his marriage-minded mother and aunt kept throwing "suitable girls" in his face during the reception. He made his toast to the happy couple and bailed before the garter toss. No way in hell he was going to fall for that trap. Braxton was happy for Bechet. He and Isis were a cute little power couple, but that didn't mean Braxton wanted anything to do with settling down now. Same as he hadn't been bothered to do so after Baron married his soon-to-be ex, Christine, either.

Not that he never planned to settle. Just not with anyone who was more concerned about his family money and his ties to the influential Westmoore family, than they were about just being with him. He was the second son; he wasn't inheriting shit from the Cross side because that wasn't how that worked, and he'd blown through what little money his mother had set aside for him in his younger, more reckless, college years. What money he did have was earned. Hard earned and he'd be damned if he ended up like Baron, blindsided by infidelity and saddled with debt over some wet pussy.

No, Braxton was content to sow his wild oats when the opportunity arose. He didn't have time to give some debutante false hope of landing a big fish to wrap her in furs and diamonds. His plan had been to change out of his monkey suit and hit up a random bar far, from anyone that moved in those so-called 'respectable' circles, or would recognize who he was. He'd deviated from his mission to buy the woman dressed as Carmen San Diego a drink. The Corinthian was a classy place, not exactly where you would go looking for a hook up, and especially not the kind of hook-up that he craved if he wanted to remain discrete. He'd learned quick that if he had any chance of continuing a casual lifestyle without interference meant keeping his shit out of the rumor mill and gossip rags as much as possible.

There was only one place like that in town, and family loyalty meant he couldn't even look at K Hotel. He knew, without a doubt, that he could have his needs met there, and in a discreet fashion, but it wasn't an option. So, a random bar hook-up, in a less flashy part of town, was his only other choice. But he hadn't counted on seeing Carmen San Diego, come to life, sitting in the lounge. He certainly hadn't expected her to be so damn cute, as she blatantly perused his disheveled post-wedding look.

He'd planned to be more subtle with his come-on, easing her into some small talk before the dirty talk in his bed. She looked like she would totally be down for a hotel rendezvous. Hell, she had definitely dressed for the fucking attention. Her trench coat did a good job of covering her body, but it couldn't hide her curves, or the sensuality that she oozed. He'd managed to catch a glimpse of what was underneath when he'd gotten close enough to peer down the gap at the collar; nothing but warm brown flesh and black lace. His dick had gone so hard, he found himself dropping his key and his room number before hightailing it out of there, not trusting himself to stay and not ravish her right then and there.

Now here he was, looking like a fool, waiting by the elevators for her. He'd seen her drop his key off at the front desk so Braxton knew he should leave the woman alone. Still, when the drunk and overly perfumed party girls started flirting his way, he eased himself next to Carmen San Diego and slid his arm around her waist. She tensed at his touch, but the elevator was too crowded for her to move out of his grasp. Braxton dropped his arm even as the crowd pushed them closer together.

Get a grip man. She isn't interested.

The drunken women burst into another fit of giggles. Their alcohol loosened bodies taking up more space than necessary as they cackled. One double over, her hips bumping Carmen against Braxton. He tensed this time as the move pressed her firmly against his chest, her coat gaping at the collar and revealing more of her delectable cleavage to him. Her delicate fingers splayed across his chest.

She tried to push away but was jostled right back into him. This time when he wrapped his arms around her waist to steady her, she didn't flinch or try to move away. She looked up at him, heat in her gaze, her lower lip caught between her teeth. Maybe she wasn't as disinterested as he thought. The elevator slowed and the doors opened.

"I believe this is your floor!" One of the drunken women spoke a little too loudly. Carmen blinked before hastily turning to leave.

That should have been the end of it but just before the elevator doors closed, Braxton found himself rushing out after her. He reached for her hand to stop her. "Wait!"

She turned around, her eyes wide with shock before she crossed her arms over her chest. "Thank you for buying my drinks, but you need to stop," she said.

"I sure as hell do, but I can't seem to make myself," he admitted.

She cocked her head to the side. Her intense gaze traveled over his body, making him feel so incredibly small despite the fact he could easily blend in with the largest of football players or bodybuilders.

"Do I need to call security? The cops?"

"No, I would never force myself on a woman. Can I walk you to your door though? I promise I won't push to come inside."

She gave him a look that assured him that she didn't believe him for one second. Hell, at this point, he didn't believe his own damn self. He was already acting so out of character, putting himself and his family at great risk if this went sideways.

"Fine," she said, and he smiled before taking her proffered hand and walking her down the hall. Her room wasn't far from the elevator. It was next to the ice maker and laundry room.

He knew the Corinthian kept a few less luxury accommodations for travelers who wanted to feel like they were living it up, without shelling out their life savings to do so. It was clear this floor was earmarked for that. He was a little curious to see what the budget accommodations looked like. He'd hand carved the mock-ups for the furniture in the luxury suites but the contract The Corinthian had with Cross Furniture hadn't extended to their economy rooms.

She pulled out her room key and turned to face him, before she did the last thing he would have expected her to do. She reached up, grabbing the back of his neck, and pulled him down to kiss him. Her full lips pressing gently against his for a few seconds before she pulled away. Despite the almost chaste nature of the kiss, her brown eyes were molten hot, her breathing quick and shallow. His dick was hard as granite once again, and he swooped in, pressing her against her room door, taking her mouth, only this time both tongue and teeth got involved with the party.

Carmen should never have kissed him. She had no idea why she'd done it. It had been a last-minute lapse in judgment. She thought that if she kissed him, she'd realize that there wasn't anything between them that she couldn't provide for herself in her own bed. Boy, had she been wrong. A simple press of lips, and she was all flushed, hot, and bothered over a stranger she didn't even know the name of.

Then he'd kissed her back, pressed her against the door of her hotel room, devouring her with a mind-melting kiss. She kissed him back, meeting him tongue to tongue, licking, sucking, probing. His massive hands slid down and hooked under her knees. He lifted her off the ground. She wrapped her legs as best she could around his thick waist as her body moved on its own, hips grinding against the massive length pressed against her dripping wet folds. The feel of his soft suit and granite cock on her bare pussy was almost too much.

"Fuck," she groaned into his mouth as her orgasm tore through her.

He stilled, pressing hard into her as she rode the waves of her orgasm with reckless abandon. Her entire body melted into his, sated and a little embarrassed. He continued to kiss her but let her legs fall from his waist. Once she was firmly back on her feet, he pulled away just enough to see the massive wet spot on the front of his pants.

"Naughty girl, you've made quite the mess," he growled.

"Sorry," Carmen squeaked out.

He closed the distance between them and kissed her again. "Don't ever apologize for coming all over me," he said.

"I just, we shouldn't have...."

Her stranger cut her off with another kiss. "Tell me to go right now, and I'll walk my ass up to my room wearing your release like a badge of honor. Then I'll fuck my hand to the smell of you and wish I was buried deep in your sweetness instead of alone. Or," and here he smiled at her, sinfully sweet, "you can pick your room or mine..."

Carmen groaned, knowing that she should definitely tell this man to kick rocks. But as amazing as her orgasm had been, it sure as hell wasn't enough to sate her appetite, nor would anything she could do on her lonesome in her hotel room. She slipped her key into the lock, then grabbed the front of his shirt to drag him inside with her.

"I need to call you something. It doesn't have to be your real name," she found herself saying as she rode his massive cock for the third time that night.

The first two times, she'd been satisfied just screaming out her climax. Now that he'd turned her into an insatiable madwoman, she needed something more from him. He sat up and latched onto her exposed nipple, pressing his hips down with his palms and settling her into a slow grind.

"Fuck, if you're gonna scream any name while on my dick that isn't the creator himself, it sure as hell is going to be mine," He hissed.

"Well, tell me quick, cuz I'm not going to last like this," Carmen gasped, gripping his shoulders to get the leverage she needed to add a little bounce to her movements. As much as she loved him grinding on her clit, she needed that extra smack to the nerve endings at the back of her pussy.

She was close, so close, and right before she flew over the edge, he gave her his name.

"Braxton, fuck, my name is Braxton."

His grip on her loosened, and she let herself go, riding him hard and rough as she cried out his name over and over before collapsing onto his chest. He flipped her onto her back taking over where she left off, ramming his dick into her so hard the headboard slammed into the wall. The wood split in two, and the new sharp edge smashed the wall behind it. He didn't stop even as more plaster rained down onto them.

"Braxton!" she cried, both out of pleasure and in concern for how insanely focused he was on fucking the life out of her pussy while the walls literally crumbled around them.

"Fuck. Yes, I love the sound of my name on your lips," he growled.

He pressed her legs wider, jack-hammering into her before pulling out completely and slipping down to suck her clit. Her legs clamped tight around his ears, her back arching as Braxton's tongue fucked her already oversensitive clit.

"Fuck, fuck, Braxton! You're...I'm...shit...Braxton!" She screamed as another orgasm tore through her.

He reared up, sliding his cock back into her pulsing core. "Mine!" he growled before spilling into the condom. He held her trapped under his body, kissing any and every exposed piece of flesh he could reach without uncoupling from her.

Carmen was sleeping beneath him, her soft, even breathing in sharp juxtaposition to his desperate haggard breath. He forced himself to roll over and slid the used condom from his dick before tying it and tossing it into the trash can beside the bed. Braxton was already growing again, thinking about another round, but this condom had been his last. He would have to make a trip to his room to get more.

He let out a slow breath. He prided himself on his sexual prowess and high libido but he'd never been this quick to recover. Once maybe, but not three times in a row. Carmen had bewitched him from the moment he set eyes on her; had turned him into a sex-crazed deviant with the fire that danced behind her eyes. She squirmed against him, her soft skin brushing against the carpet of hair that covered his chest. He shifted slightly so he could cradle her closer.

This feels right.

The impulsive thought drifted through his mind as he studied what features he could in the dimly lit room. Her heart-shaped face was pressed into his side, but he had a feeling her face was one he would never forget. Her al-mond-shaped eyes had grown wide with wonder at the first flick of his tongue on her clit. The way her eyebrows pinched together and her lush mouth fell open when he'd slid inside for the first time.

Her once bone-straight hair was beginning to curl into loose ringlets. Absently, he twirled a strand around his finger before letting it fall back into place. That's when he noticed the flecks of white paint and plaster that decorated the both of them like flecks of confetti. Braxton glanced up at the gaping hole and split headboard and swore. He would definitely be paying for her to change rooms. On second thought, it would be better if he convinced her to move to his room.

That was if they were allowed to stay in the hotel after the mess he'd made, VIP or not. He sat up, white flakes of plaster falling from his hair. He was careful not to disturb Carmen in her slumber, maybe he could handle everything before having to wake her. He didn't want to ruin their time together with arguments about who would pay for the damages. Of course, maybe she wouldn't want to stay with him now that she was thoroughly satisfied.

Fuck! I hope she wants more.

There was a knock on the door. Braxton sighed and reached for his pants. He wasn't surprised at all to see the hotel manager and security when he opened the door.

"Sir, we've had several noise complaints from other guests," the manager said.

Braxton nodded and spoke up before the manager could officially kick them out. "Yeah, sorry about that. Give me a second to get dressed, and I'll come down to check out," he said and shut the door before the manager could say anything more.

He found his shirt and called his cousin Dom. Between the wedding and some writers convention happening, there was almost no chance of finding a decent room somewhere else in town. He also wasn't about to bring a hook up anywhere near his family so that meant calling in a favor with his burgeoning real estate mogul cousin.

"This better be an emergency," Dom growled.

"Fuck yeah, it is. Do you have any furnished properties I can crash at for the rest of the weekend?"

"Yeah," he said.

"Cool, can you send me the address? I can meet you there in about an hour."

Dominic didn't immediately answer. Braxton could hear his cousin filling in his girlfriend Sinai before he finally did.

"I'm busy, but Elias has a copy of the keys. I'll send him to meet you," Dom said.

"Cool, thanks, man. I owe you," Braxton said and hung up.

He finished getting dressed and closed up Carmen's suitcase. Thankfully she wasn't one of those people who completely unpacked at hotel rooms. Aside from her toiletries and the Carmen San Diego get-up, everything else was neatly organized and packed up in a single small suitcase. Almost like she had either just arrived or hadn't planned to stay in the room long.

He gently shook her awake. "Carmen, love. We gotta get going."

She blinked a few times before groaning and rolling away from him. With a sigh, he lifted her out of bed, and she glared at him.

"What are you doing?"

"We got kicked out of the hotel. Don't worry, I'll cover all the expenses, but we've got to change hotels."

"Fuck; are you serious?"

"Yep, now come on. Put your coat back on, and let's blow this popsicle stand."

She looked like she would fuss more, but instead, she slipped back into her boots and coat. Her pretty lace undergarments lay in pieces on the floor, so she didn't bother with those. Braxton got her and her bags to the elevator, a short trip up to his own room where she collapsed on the couch while he gathered his own things.

He wasn't nearly as neat and organized as she was, but he also hadn't brought much with him to begin with. The manager shook his head as Braxton carried Carmen half-asleep to the front desk to check out. Then it was out to his rental car and off to the upscale warehouse studio his cousin Dom kept as a model home for his district revitalization project.

It was another business opportunity to show off Cross furniture's range in design, yet it was one that neither he or

Bechet had pushed. The Cross' and the Westmoores' didn't mix business with family like that. Braxton couldn't blame them, given the Cross Family legacy was the antithesis of everything the Westmoores stood for. How his mother had ever married his father was a mystery both sides of the family had yet to decipher. Love wouldn't have been enough to bridge not only the physical distance between the two families but the social one as well.

With Carmen sleeping soundly next to him in his rental car, Braxton headed to the address his cousin had given him. It wasn't a very long drive but it gave Braxton a bit of time to get his head together. First, the gorgeous Carmen San Diego. He didn't even know her real name, had no idea how long she would be in town either. Whatever happened between them was temporary and he needed to nip the budding feelings that had sprouted sometime in the last hour or so, before they bloomed and he was up shit creek. He was already pushing it turning this one night into more, taking her to a second location when he should have just given her his room and gone to stay with one of his cousins.

Second, the owners of the Corinthian were going to be pissed once they found out about the damage he caused. Yet, their anger was nothing compared to the disgust he felt about the quality of their economy rooms. Maybe he could talk with the owners about adding their rooms to the scope of their contract, at a steep discount. He was slightly offended at how cheap they'd gone with the furnishings there, when Braxton had put a lot of heart into the craftmanship of the furniture in the luxury rooms above. That and the fact that perhaps it might keep the family from being banned from yet another luxury hotel chain.

If that did come to pass, maybe Bechet would be up to adding another branch to the Cross Logging tree and start their own hotel chain. Braxton chuckled, that would never happen. The Crosses were running short of male figureheads as it was. Baron had Cross Logging, Bechet had Cross Furniture. Braxton liked being in his workshop more than dealing with business. His cousin Hunter wasn't exactly looking to be locked into the family business either.

The rest of the Cross men were either dead, crazy or lifelong mountain men who didn't care about much more than swinging an axe and living off the grid. So yeah, further expansion was not in the works. He just had to hope that his lapse of judgment and lack of control when it came to his Carmen didn't put him and his brother's dreams further behind.

His Carmen? Shit. He really needed to get a grip.

The GPS announced that they had arrived at their destination. Carmen didn't stir as the car slowed to a stop, and Braxton thought it best not to bother her while he handled things with his cousin. It would also help keep Braxton's business out of the family rumor mill. It was already going to be an issue that he'd called in a favor with Dom so last minute. The last thing he wanted was for there to be added rumors of him spending time with a woman, especially when there was nothing to report; or at least, nothing to report that would make his mother happy or get her off his back about settling down and giving her grandchildren.

Dom's younger brother, Elias, met Braxton at the door, a scowl on his face. "Man, here's the keys. You and Dom both owe me for this," he said before walking off to his own car.

Braxton opened the door before going back to get Carmen. She was still sleeping, her hat discarded in the back of his rental car leaving her angelic features exposed in the dim lighting of the street. Something shifted in his chest, Braxton wasn't sure what exactly but he felt a literal shift before the urge to care for and protect Carmen came over him. He eased her out of the front seat careful not to wake her. Her warm body pressed against his chest as he cradled her in his arms.

He took every precaution not to wake her as he moved up the concrete stairs to the front door and across the threshold. Braxton hadn't been in this new layout of his cousin's development but thankfully everything was laid out in a very functional and intuitive way. He adjusted Carmen in his arms as he moved through the open concept living area to the hallway where the bedrooms would be.

The doors to the rooms were open so he didn't have to jostle Carmen around to reach door handles. He passed the first room which was designed to be an office space, and another that was set up to be a guest room before reaching the master suite. Braxton took Carmen straight to the king-sized bed. Thankfully it was a real bed and not a fake one made of cardboard like most staged homes used.

Carmen stirred a little as he pulled back the covers and placed her on the mattress. Her tiny fingers clutching to his shirt. He gently pried her hand free before kissing each of her finger tips. She moaned and or a second Braxton contemplated waking her up to continue seducing her. He let go of her hand and finished tucking her in. He would be patient this once and allow her to rest while he went back for their bags.

The cool night air and break from Carmen's tempting body gave Braxton's mind time to process just what the hell he was doing. He was acting completely out of character but for the life of him, Braxton couldn't find fault in his actions. All he knew was that he wasn't done with Carmen yet. The best he could hope for in this scenario was that she felt the same when she woke up, and that she didn't have an early flight. According to the front desk, she had only rented the room for the night. Which didn't bode well for Braxton on that front. He'd have to ask her later, and if need be pay for the change in her plans.

With their things inside Braxton secured the front door and sent a quick thank you text to Dom. He didn't expect the man to answer at this hour but he did.

D: Just remember to put the key back in the lockbox when you're done with your rendezvous. Try not to break anything. I'll send the invoice for the cleanup.

Braxton snorted and tucked his phone back in his pocket. Maybe Dom wasn't as removed from the gossip circles as Braxton thought. The last thing Braxton needed was for any of this to become gossip fodder but it was too late to worry about that now. The wheels were already in motion. Plus, Braxton had little interest in pressing the breaks where Carmen was concerned.

He rolled their bags into the bedroom and tried not to think of the consequences of his actions as he stripped out his clothes and got into bed with her. Carmen rolled over and snuggled into him, her head on his chest. The move almost made him forget that Carmen herself was a huge variable in all of this. It wouldn't be the first time a woman gamed her way into a rich man's bed for social or monetary gain. For a brief moment, Braxton contemplated if he was being played. If she had marked him from the start and her reluctance at first had all been an act to sucker him in. No, his Carmen, despite being up for whatever he'd thrown at her in bed, was too innocent for that. She herself had said she wasn't the casual hook-up type and nothing about her behavior had hinted at the contrary. Braxton wrapped his arms around her and let sleep claim him. Whatever the outcome, he could worry about it in the morning. For now, they both needed the rest.

Chapter 2

Carmen only vaguely remembered the drive from the hotel to what she assumed was Braxton's apartment. She couldn't tell. Wherever Braxton had taken her was definitely not another hotel. It might have been a timeshare home with its sterile but homey décor, because it sure didn't fit the brusque mountain of a man who'd spent the last few hours fucking her brains out.

"Sorry I didn't exactly give you a tour," Braxton said setting a cup of coffee down in front of her.

He was shirtless, his broad chest on full display, the sun glinting off the thick golden-brown curls that carpeted his thick muscled frame before disappearing into the stretch waistband of his grey sweatpants. The curls all but obscured the man's muscles, but she'd had the pleasure of discovering each and every sharp line and hard plane underneath. Real muscles, the kind earned through hard manual labor, not hours in a gym.

"Oh, but this place has wonderful ceilings!" she exclaimed.

"Just ceilings?"

"Oh, and the carpet in front of the fireplace has a wonderfully intricate design, and it's so soft and thick," she licked her lips and Braxton groaned.

"Babe, I'm trying to be nice and feed you before I fuck you on this counter," he said.

"What, you can't multitask?" Carmen giggled and took a sip of the coffee.

"Woman," Braxton said before rounding the counter, his hard dick bobbing beneath the thin grey fabric, a different kind of hunger in his eyes. Carmen slipped off the barstool at the counter and met him halfway. She sank to her knees, dragging his pants down to his ankles and freeing his erection. She didn't wait for him to ask, just flicked her tongue out briefly catching the head of him. A tentative taste before she sank him into her mouth.

"Fuck, please tell me you don't have to leave in an hour or some shit," he said.

Carmen's reply was to take him deeper. She didn't want to talk about when she was leaving because that would only bring up thoughts about what the hell she was going to do when she did. Her flight was due to leave the following morning, and she didn't want to waste a second of the time she had left to enjoy Braxton. She would enjoy this much more pleasurable escape into the sex bubble they'd created. Safe from the shame, judgment and strings of the real world.

Braxton's hand gripped the back of her head. Not tight, but with a definite possessiveness as he began to fuck her mouth. Carmen had hoped to be able to control this encounter with him; drive him to the brink of insanity, the way he had done to her over and over again. Yet, she found herself giving in, relaxing into his rhythm. Her gaze flicked up, expecting a closed-eyed grimace, a deep concentration on reaching his own release. But her eyes met his wide open, staring down at her with a mix of awe and ecstasy. His thighs began to quake and he leaned against the counter as if he knew he wouldn't be able to hold himself up any longer. Carmen swirled her tongue around his length, suctioning her cheeks tighter as he increased his pace.

"I'm going to blow," he said between clenched teeth.

He let go of her head and slid out of her mouth. Carmen kept her kneeling position in front of him as he gripped his base and finished himself off, his release coating his hand and lower abdomen.

"You okay?" she asked after a few moments.

Braxton sank to the floor with her, laughing. "Give me a sec."

"Sure." Carmen started to get up but he grabbed her arm and pulled her against his chest.

"Fuck, I've never been a cuddler and I know I should get cleaned up first," Braxton said. "But I just want to hold you after that."

Carmen relaxed into his embrace. Something about his exasperation made her feel all warm and fuzzy inside. Like this was something more than just a weekend fling. Maybe that's why she asked the first personal question between them. "What do you like to do for fun?"

Braxton pressed a soft kiss to her forehead. "You mean other than making you scream my name?"

"Yes, like hobbies."

"I like the outdoors. Hiking, fishing, rock climbing," he said.

Carmen couldn't help the snort that followed her short guffaw of laughter. "I'm sorry. I just. Do you know you totally look the mountain man type? I shouldn't be surprised."

To be honest, Carmen had thought he was into some kind of extreme sport. The scarring on Braxton's back could easily have come from a rock-climbing fall but they were still too much of strangers for her to feel comfortable asking about it.

"Well, going by looks you seem like the school teacher type. I bet your hobbies are baking and making macaroni crafts," he snarked.

Carmen sat up and shook her head. "You would be dead wrong on that. I actually enjoy the outdoors as well, but more from the photographer's point of view."

"Oh really? You one of those social media influencers?"

"No, I just like capturing nature in all its glory. If I had more time, I'd be on the trails all the time but portrait photography is what's paying the bills right now," she sighed.

"Is that what brought you to Mulberry? Portrait work?"

Carmen settled back against his chest, not wanting to look into his eyes as she blatantly lied to him. "No, I just came for a visit. A break from the daily grind. What brings you to Mulberry?"

"My brother's wedding. I was just returning to my room from the reception when I saw you in the hotel bar," Braxton said.

"So, weddings, do they like do it for you? You get all wound up over people pledging themselves to a life happily ever after?"

Braxton snorted. "Marriage ain't a guarantee of happiness. My oldest brother is miserable as shit because of his marriage. I have higher hopes for this brother's marriage but no I definitely don't get off on people getting hitched. The opposite. I bailed halfway through the reception to avoid all the horny singles," he said.

"Wow, I have so many questions but let's keep this light. Tell me about this rock climbing. I mean, do you go shirtless?"

"Shirtless? That's what you want to know about it? Not if I go free climbing?"

"Is that like free balling?" Carmen almost didn't finish the question before she was laughing again. Braxton joined in on the laughter, setting the tone for the rest of their conversation. They eventually moved from the floor and managed to feed themselves before Braxton suggested they take advantage of the massive shower.

"I'll join you in a second," Carmen said as they reached the bedroom.

She'd spotted her purse and realized she hadn't been in touch with anyone since last night. The girls were probably worried about her. She checked her phone for the first time since leaving the bar at the hotel. She had a million texts from the girls asking her where the hell she was. As well as a few texts from Noah saying how much he missed her and wished she could be there with him. She deleted those before texting her girls back.

Group Text Amayah, Scarlett, Imena

C: Sorry I've been off-grid. Decided to try climbing the mountain.

Within seconds she got a reply

S: Get it, girl!

A: You better be wearing a fucking harness, Ms. Mountain Climber

Imena just texted wide eyes and a mountain emoji.

C: It's been a fun climb but I won't be missing my flight for the view. I'll give details when I return.

S: You better.

With a shake of her head, Carmen switched over to her email to double-check her itinerary. She had just a few hours left of her sex bubble before returning to reality. A small part of her wished she could just stay Carmen San Diego forever, because she was obviously a much cooler person than Carmen Quinn the pushover. Despite how amazingly this man fucked, or how much they both enjoyed outdoor sports, there was no way this was lasting beyond this weekend. He'd never even asked her what her name is. He had just kept calling her Carmen because of her stupid outfit. It didn't matter if that was her real name. He didn't know that.

She was just setting down her phone when Braxton emerged from the bathroom.

"If you needed a break, you could have just told me," he said startling her.

She rolled to her side, staring up at him from her perch on the bed. She'd sprawled out to get comfortable as she'd gone through her messages. She gestured to her naked body and smirked. "I had planned to join you but I had a few things to handle first," she said.

His hazel eyes traveled over her body with adoration before they darkened with the telltale signs of sexual hunger. The towel around his waist tented almost immediately before he dropped it to the floor. "I need to handle a few things myself," he growled before crossing to the bed. He grabbed her by the waist and pulled her to the edge of the bed. "I owe you for this morning."

Carmen knew exactly where this was headed and part of her wanted to beg off. The brief break had been enough to put a small damper on her enthusiasm for ignoring reality. She also really needed a shower and a nap, but she wasn't about to pass up on another round of multiple orgasms. Who knew when she would get this again after this moment? She needed to stock up for the dry months ahead of her.

"For the blowjob?" Carmen gasped as his thumb circled her clit. "If we are really keeping tabs on orgasms, that only scratched the surface of the debt I owe you."

"Then I'll collect payment in the form of licks on this sweet pussy of yours. Ten licks per orgasm is a fair price, I'd say."

He dove between her legs before she could even begin to make sense of that statement. Her hands gripped his hair and held him right where she needed him.

"Fuck, what happens when I orgasm on your mouth?"

"Then I'll have to claim payment on those as well," he chuckled, the soft puffs of warm air against her bare flesh pushing her closer to the edge.

Heaven. That was the only word adequate enough to describe the way being with Carmen felt. It didn't matter if it was his nose buried between her lower lips or her mouth wrapped around his cock. Every moment was a little slice of heaven. Maybe that was why he didn't balk at the idea of her taking control for the rest of the evening. After he'd reclaimed the orgasm debt, they'd taken a relaxing bath together. Chatted about hiking and her photography. Then, as he'd lotioned her up, she'd made these adorable little purring noises and expressed her wish to tie him up.

Any other woman he would have laughed and distracted her with another orgasm but he'd found himself intrigued by the idea. Carmen was currently tying his hands to the headboard with a pair of his silk socks. Her naked body, so close and yet just out of reach enough to prevent him from regaining any sort of upper hand.

Braxton never relinquished control in the bedroom. It was rule number one in not letting a fling get the wrong idea. Then again, nothing he'd done with Carmen so far had been by his unofficial fuckboy rule book. He'd broken all the rules from the beginning. First, in not taking no for an answer when she'd turned down his initial offer at the bar. Then again by moving to a second location and extending their time together from one night to two. The only talking allowed during a fling was to get consent, to set the ground rules, and dirty talk to keep the party going.

Carmen is different.

The thought set off a moment of panic that was quickly overshadowed by the fact that one of Carmen's nipples grazed the top of his lip. He caught it in his mouth and suckled, eliciting a moan from her that erased any further deep dives into how he was going against the rules he'd lived by for the last ten years.

Her body sank against his, "Keep sucking."

He grinned as she arched against him, positioning her dripping core over his lap before sinking onto his condom-clad erection. Her slick heat engulfed him and he tugged at his binding. The need to touch her, to guide her hips as she ground down against him was overwhelming. It was exquisite torture as she used his body to bring herself so close to the edge, but never enough to send either of them flying over.

Every time he thought she would put them both out of their misery, allow either of them the release their bodies craved, she would switch up positions. Raise the bar on the amount of pleasure that one could have in any one sexual encounter, giving him a new view, a new sensation, a new perspective, on what pleasure could be.

His dick was so hard it was bordering on painful. He was panting and writhing, on a brink of a heart attack from the intensity of it all, when she finally let go, her movements becoming erratic, her cries of pleasure mixed with an almost maniacal laughter and Braxton was right there with her.

He yanked his hands free and pulled her flush against his body, capturing her screams with his mouth as he lost all control. He pounded into her, releasing himself in a deafening roar.

"Mine!"

Braxton was snoring away beside her in bed. It was the first time since they met that she hadn't woken up to his dick, hands or mouth already on her. Granted, last night had been the first night he'd allowed her to take control. She'd tied him to the bed with a pair of his silk socks and rode him in at least six different positions before they'd both passed out from the intensity of their joint orgasm. So yeah, he was spent and so was she, but reality beckoned.

She tried to slip out of his hold but his grip on her tightened.

"Mine," he muttered in his sleep.

If only things were simpler. If the circumstances were different.

It didn't matter. She couldn't stay. She didn't belong here or with him. Carmen had reached the end of her weekend reprieve; it was time she got back and handled the wreck that was her actual life. She tugged a pillow between her and Braxton and managed to slip away, leaving it in her place. Thankfully, the place Braxton had absconded her to in the middle of the night was close to the airport. She had just enough time to shower and have one last longing look at the man who had given her a sexual awakening to remember before she left.

It was only when she reached the airport that she began to regret not leaving a note. She wouldn't have given him a way to contact her, that would be too much but she could have at least thanked him for their time together. She shook the thought from her head. No, it was better this way. A clean break. As it was, she would have dreams of this weekend for the foreseeable future.

Carmen cleared security and grabbed a coffee on her way through the terminal for domestic flights. It wasn't until she reached her gate that reality really hit. Noah looked up from his phone for a brief second and his eyes lit up in shock.

"Carmen? What are you doing here?"

CHAPTER 3

Braxton woke up a few hours later clutching a Carmen-scented pillow to his chest. He smiled to himself, imagining her slipping the pillow in what had become her place snuggled against him. He rolled over, letting the pillow fall away. Was she in the bathroom? The thought of her naked in the shower had his already hard cock aching with anticipation of being buried inside of her again. Yet, as he looked around the room he realized Carmen and her things were gone. She hadn't even left a note.

"Fuck," he cursed.

He should have known she would pull a Houdini on him. Last night Carmen had been different, more reserved, quiet. Not when she was on his dick, but in the arguably less intimate moments. Yesterday they had chatted about crazy hiking stories and the weirdest photoshoots she'd done while soaking in the tub together. It was the only time he got a glimpse at the real woman behind her Carmen San Diego vibe.

You let a real one slip away. All that potential, a waste.

He cleaned up and threw on some clothes. He didn't even have time to dwell on how bad he fucked up this time. He should have asked Carmen her real name. Could have snuck a peek at her phone or wallet, anything to give him a clue about her. Hell, he should have paid more attention when checking them out of the hotel, her name had surely been on the room information, but he couldn't just go back there asking about her.

His phone buzzed in his pocket.

"Hey, cuz. Where you at? The flight leaves in an hour," Hunter said.

"Fuck. I might not make this flight. Tell Ma not to freak out if I don't make it," Braxton said.

"This have anything to do with the red dress you holed up with at one of Dom's places?"

Braxton would ask where his cousin had heard about that, but it was no secret that Elias was a fucking gossip. Elias had probably seen Carmen sleeping in his rental and spread the news. Elias and Hunter were two peas in a pod so it was no surprise that Hunter would be one of the first he spilled the beans to. You'd think the two of them were related, instead of just sharing mutual cousins.

"Don't say anything or I'll tell everyone about your little side-piece in Sowell."

"You wouldn't."

"I sure as hell would," Braxton said, putting the key in the lockbox by the door.

"You'd really out me?" Hunter hissed.

Braxton pinched the bridge of his nose. Hunter's horror wasn't at the idea that the family would find out that he was seeing a guy – they all knew he was bisexual already – no, he was pissed because, just like Braxton, if anyone in the family got any hint that he was dating someone seriously, it would only be a matter of time before talks about wedding bells and babies would start. It was something neither cousin was interested in. At least, not in the near future.

Though if you hadn't screwed things up with Carmen, maybe...

Braxton didn't allow his brain to finish that thought. Whatever could have come from this weekend no longer matter. Carmen had ghosted him. For all he knew what he thought he'd felt growing between them both had been all one-sided, a side effect of being around a blissfully happy couple for their wedding.

"All I'm saying is that I'd put a bug in their ear that those trips you make to the other side of the mountain ain't all business. Then you'd get your own taste of the wedding pressure."

"Fine, whatever, just get your ass home safe," Hunter hung up.

The only thing working in Braxton's favor was that the warehouse district was way closer to the airport than Corinthian had been. He dropped the keys of his rental car into the quick drop and ran through security. Due to the nature of his family's business, travel was a necessity, so he'd made sure to have TSA pre-check and every other amenity to get him through the airport quickly. Between that and a convenient delay of the flight, Braxton made it to the plane just before they closed the doors.

Hunter shot him a disgusted look as he took his seat next to him in first class. The family could afford a private jet, but Wilhelm Cross refused to have anything to do with that level of luxury. He wasn't a miser, he just thought most of the trappings of wealth a waste. Flying first class was a compromise for their high society-raised mother, Melinda. Then they'd all get in their trucks and drive the two hours to the Cross Estate in Edgewood.

Braxton did notice that Baron wasn't on the plane with them. He tapped Hunter on the shoulder to get his attention. "Where's Baron?"

Hunter shrugged. "He sent a text saying he was staying behind but didn't give a reason."

Braxton nodded and Hunter went back to listening to his music. He hoped his older brother stayed behind to get rid of his ex-wife Christine for good, not because he was taking her lying, gold-digging ass back. That whole relationship was a shit show. It had almost threatened to ruin Bechet's big day when Christine crashed the wedding. That woman sure knew how to throw a fuss.

Baron had sat there drinking himself into a stupor until Braxton had the bartender at the open bar cut him off. He'd pulled his brother to the side and told him he needed to man up where his wife was concerned. The both of them could only use grief as an excuse for not dealing with their marital problems for so long. Although, how anyone could put a timeline on the grief of losing a child was beyond him. After dealing with that mess, Braxton had left the reception and run into Carmen.

Enough. We're worried about your brother here. Not some broad who ghosted you.

Pulling out his phone he shot Baron a quick text.

B: Hey, Bro. You're not on the plane.

BigBro: Handling some long overdue business. Be home in a few days.

B: Let me know if you need anything. You know like a shovel and a conveniently body-sized hole high up in the mountains.

BigBro: Fuck, Brax. You know you shouldn't be joking about shit like that.

B: Who says I'm joking. With everything that bitch put you and our family through.

BigBro: Enjoy your flight. Don't choke on those dry-ass airline snacks.

Braxton knew that was the end of that conversation. Especially as the announcement was made for them to turn off all devices in preparation for takeoff. He turned off his phone and got as comfortable as he could in the tiny airplane seats. A man of his size dwarfed even the relatively large first class accommodations. Thankfully, the droning on by his mother and father about how awesome Bechet's wedding had been, was enough to put him right to sleep.

Five hours nonstop to Sowell City Airport, he managed to sleep through the entire flight. Hunter punched his arm to wake him up when it was time to deboard, then he and his family headed down to baggage claim. He hadn't needed to check a bag but being the gentleman his mother raised him to be, he waited to collect his mother's luggage. His family stood nearby chatting away about Bechet's wedding and whether or not Bechet and Isis would spend the holidays in Mulberry or Edgewood.

Braxton did his best to tune them out, picking up on others' conversations until he heard her voice drifting over the constant chatter of his family. At first, he thought it was just his mind playing tricks on him, but then he heard it again, raised not in passion but in anger. He turned to see her in jeans and a t-shirt, her natural curls tied up in a puff at the top of her head. He'd been pleasantly surprised to see her natural hair after he'd made her sweat out whatever straightening she'd done to get her hair flat, like the character she was playing. Only now it wasn't her appearance that kept his eyes glued to her. It was the scene she was causing.

"I already told you there is no discussion to be had, Noah. This isn't the first time you've cheated. The difference now is that I'm not ignorant enough to let you get away with it. I'm done! Should have been done ages ago!"

"Calm your ass down, we'll talk about this at home," the man she had been yelling at said. He grabbed her arm and she winced. Braxton hadn't realized he was moving until he was right on them.

"Get your hands off her," he growled.

"Look buddy, this is between me and my woman," Noah said.

"I'm not your woman," Carmen said just as Braxton said, "She ain't your woman, she's mine."

Carmen looked up at Braxton. The second their eyes met sent a jolt of arousal straight to Braxton's dick. He'd feel ashamed if it weren't for the same glint of arousal beneath the shock in Carmen's gaze.

"This why you're trippin? You fucking this backwoods asshole behind my back?" Noah spat.

Braxton pulled Carmen out of Noah's grasp and hauled her against him. "She sure the fuck is so move along asshole," Braxton said.

She should pull away from Braxton, stand up for herself, do *something* to challenge Noah. What that would be? Carmen had no idea, but she definitely hadn't expected things to turn out like this. She'd sat next to Noah on the flight home. She'd done it on purpose when she had decided to surprise him. He'd been surprised to see her at the gate and she hadn't wanted to risk getting kicked off the overbooked flight by causing a scene. So, she'd held off on dropping the bomb on him until they were back in Sowell City. Making up an excuse about a misguided attempt at reconnecting with her parents. Even that had been a mistake; they'd whisper-argued for the first hour of the flight about her fake failed attempt to reconnect with her family, but she'd been too tired to continue. She'd fallen asleep letting him think she was content to just have him in her life.

When they landed, she'd done her best to try and keep calm until they could get to the privacy of their shared condo. It would give her more time to formulate her parting words and arrange to stay with Imena until she could get a new place. She hadn't meant to blow up at him in the middle of the airport but then Noah had touched her. She flinched away from him, he'd called her out on it, and she lost it. There was no way she could pretend any longer. The flight had been long enough. It was one thing to know he'd been with others when they were on breaks or broken up, it was another now that they had been dating for two straight years and lived together.

Of all the things she expected to happen during her public blowup, Braxton coming to her rescue wasn't one of them. Now, here she stood between her weekend fling and her now ex-boyfriend making an even bigger scene as more and more people gathered.

Noah was pissed, he'd been angry before but not like this.

"I'm not doing this here," he snapped before storming off.

Carmen could only gape at his retreating form. Braxton turned her to face him and made her look him in the eye. "Tell me you weren't in love with that asshole. Tell me what we had wasn't just revenge fucking," he said.

Carmen swallowed hard. "I did love him once, and I'm sorry but you're right," she admitted.

She waited for him to walk away. To call her a whore or something along those lines. Instead, he kissed her. "I'll take you to get your stuff. Make sure he doesn't try to pull some shit while you do. Then you and I are gonna have a little chat," he said.

He didn't give her a chance to argue or back out this time. Instead, he held her hand tightly in his and marched her over to where his family was staring at both of them.

"I'm going to be helping my friend out this evening. Y'all don't wait up for me," he said before pulling her out of the airport and to what she assumed was his truck. It was a green F-150, with the kind of wear only a real working vehicle would have, and the logo for Cross Lumber emblazoned on the door. He tossed both their bags in the back and opened the door for her. She reluctantly climbed into the passenger seat, before pulling out her phone and updating the girls about her fallout with Noah at the airport.

Only she didn't mention Braxton. She wasn't sure why, maybe she just wanted to keep it between her and him for now, but instead, she just said a good Samaritan had offered her a ride into town.

"Where we headed?" Braxton asked after climbing into the driver's seat.

Carmen gave him the address of her and Noah's apartment. He plugged it into his phone, and then they were on the road. It was nearly an hour drive into town and then another thirty to the downtown neighborhood because of the after-church traffic.

"Carmen's your real name," he said.

Carmen nodded.

"Carmen Quinn, and you're Braxton Cross," she said.

He nodded. Hell, she should have recognized him that first night. Should have put two and two together when he mentioned the wedding, but she'd been thrown off by his lack of beard and fancy clothes. Despite the family's wealth, the Cross brothers weren't your typical fancy rich boys. Gruff bearded mountain men, with the reputation of felling hearts just as well as felling trees on the other side of Sowell Gate Mountains.

"We'll take as much as we can fit in my truck and then I'll arrange for the rest of your stuff to be picked up later. After that, we'll grab some food and talk," he said.

Carmen nodded and went into the house. As she looked around, she realized just how little of her was actually in the space. Over the years, Noah had stripped her of almost everything. She'd left so much behind just to move here with him. Two years later and the only evidence she even lived there were the framed photos she'd taken of the surrounding area and her toiletries in the bathroom. She grabbed a larger suitcase and headed to the closet. Even there, she realized there wasn't much she wanted to take.

None of the dresses Noah insisted she needed, to be seen on his arm publicly; none of the high heels that killed her feet. She emptied her underwear drawers and grabbed the clothes she actually liked wearing, and a few things she needed for work. Her gear was already in the back of her jeep so she could go hiking on a whim. Then she moved to the office and grabbed her computer. Everything else from her photography business was at her studio, a small space she rented next to Sowell Sisters Boutique and Events. Braxton was standing in the living room admiring one of her photos when she ventured back out.

"Did you take this?" he asked.

Carmen smiled. "Yeah, I didn't lie about being a photographer."

He reached up and took the picture off the wall. "You want me to take the rest of them too?" he asked.

"I was actually planning to leave them. I won't have much space even after I find a new place," Carmen said.

Braxton shook his head. "An asshole like that doesn't deserve your art," he said and proceeded to take all her photos down from the walls, before going to put them in the seat of his cab.

Carmen rolled her suitcase to her jeep and put her laptop bag in the front seat.

"How many more boxes do you think you'll need for the rest of it?" he asked.

"None. I guess I already had my foot half out the door these last two years. Didn't even bother to make myself at home despite everything," she answered.

Braxton looked at her for a moment before pulling her into his arms. "Fuck, Carmen. I want to kill that fucker for the number he did on you. You deserve so much better," he said.

"I know," she whispered before pulling out of his grasp.

They stared into each other's eyes for a moment, the tension growing thick and she ached to lean forward and close the gap between them.

"Carmen." Braxton closed his eyes, breaking eye contact.

"What we had this weekend. It was supposed to be revenge but it wasn't. I could never allow something so beautiful and real to be so fucking petty and childish. That being said. I'd very much like you to revenge-fuck me on his bed until we break the walls or the headboard. I want him to see the mess I make when you're fucking me. I want him to know that he never treated my body the way you have," she said.

Braxton's eyes flew open and he looked pissed. Carmen was about to say forget it. To apologize for being so wanton and rude when he crushed his mouth to hers.

"Show me to the bed we're about to fucking ruin," he growled.

Carmen giggled before stripping out of her jeans and t-shirt on her way up the stairs to the bedroom. The bed Carmen had shared with Noah, wasn't nearly as sturdy as the one at the hotel; it crashed to the floor within minutes of Braxton rocking her world, but he didn't stop. Oh God did he not stop as he brought her to orgasm over and over again until the bed was covered in their sweat and the results of her multiple orgasms. He'd even buried his face between her legs until she was squirting all over the place. She hadn't even known she could squirt until this weekend with Braxton.

"Fuck, we should go before he gets back. I'm surprised he hasn't shown up already," she breathed as she looked over at the toppled alarm clock.

It was already nearly 6pm and Noah wouldn't stay away for much longer. He'd probably only stayed away this long to try, and formulate the perfect argument to get her back. It wouldn't be the first time he'd done so, but this time Carmen was immune to his charm. Her pussy was too sore for her to put her jeans back on and the rest of her clothes were already packed into her car so she sauntered over to the closet and pulled out one of the few dresses she wasn't completely opposed to wearing. Coincidentally, it was also Noah's least favorite, a floor-length maxi dress with pockets. She tied it at the knee so she could walk more easily in it. Braxton shrugged into his blue Henley and boot-cut jeans before shoving his feet into a well-worn pair of tan steel-toed boots. With his full beard shining not with his cedar scented beard oil but her pussy juices, he licked his lips before sweeping her into his arms.

"Text your little friend that you won't be coming tonight. We've got a room with room service waiting on us a few blocks over," he said.

"Oh really," Carmen breathed.

"Yes, really," He said and tossed her over his shoulder.

He carried her effortlessly down the stairs setting her down only to grab the clothes she'd stripped out of, and so she could put her socks and shoes back on.

"I'll meet you at the hotel," she said moving over to her jeep which was parked in the short drive. Braxton looked like he would protest but instead he kissed her one more time before informing her that they would be staying at the Sowell City Regency.

CHAPTER 4

B raxton should feel like shit for what they'd just done, but hell if he cared at the moment. All he cared about was Carmen, and his plans to make her forget all about her loser ex. He was short on time to do it. He knew that he'd most likely have to let her go after tonight. A brief moment of panic seized him at the thought of not seeing her again, even knowing that it was for the best.

Carmen said she didn't love Noah, and all signs pointed to their fucked-up situation being done long before this weekend, but Braxton wasn't stupid. He knew what it meant to fuck a broken heart away. He could be that for Carmen now and worry about the warm fuzzies in his gut whenever he thought about her later.

He watched her pull out of the driveway and hit the road, pulling off after her leaving that house, and hopefully Noah, behind for good. He'd called ahead to the hotel while he'd waited for her to pack her things. If Braxton were a better man, he would have taken her to a restaurant to talk and then made sure she got to her friend's place safely. He was beginning to understand that he couldn't be the better man where Carmen was concerned, even if he'd never do anything to jeopardize her safety.

That blatant porn movie scenario they just acted out in her ex's bedroom was evidence of that. He was being selfish as shit, enjoying every minute she allowed him to pleasure her, and this was just the beginning. It started with fucking her brains out in her ex's bed, and would end with seducing her in the honeymoon suite at the Sowell Gate Regency.

One more night.

That was all he had to try and sate his lust for Carmen.

Carmen desperately wanted to feel some sort of shame about waltzing into the fanciest hotel in town with nothing but a purse full of condoms, but something made her almost delight in it. Braxton held her firmly against his side as he snagged their room key with a simple nod to the front desk clerk, before dragging them over to the elevator.

"Do you do this a lot?"

The question as out of her mouth before she could stop herself. Braxton pressed her against the wall of the elevator and gave her a hard look.

"You mean do I bring women to fancy hotels to fuck? I'd be lying if I said it never happened before, but most women I entertain ain't this lucky. A quick fuck in the bathroom of a bar, getting my dick sucked in a car. Maybe fucked from behind while bent over the hood of my truck. I make them feel good and send them on their way before they get any ideas in their pretty little heads about becoming anything more than a little fun," Braxton said.

"Isn't that what this is? I mean, I'm not looking for a relationship obviously. I just want to know what I'm in for," she said.

Carmen would be lying if she said his words hadn't rubbed her the wrong way. What girl would still be all hot and bothered for a man who basically admitted to being the love 'em and leave 'em type. Yet, in her case, she was already too enthralled with his intensity and that wonderfully magical dick, to have that confirmation send her running for the hills.

"To be honest, I don't know what this is. I just know it ain't that. If it was, I never would have rescued you at the airport. You aren't like the women that go out of their way to casually catch my eye. Most of them only want the fuck, and others want more from me then I have to give," he said.

Carmen bit her lip, avoiding his gaze. "Okay."

"Okay?"

"What do you want me to say, Braxton? I have shit taste in men. This was only supposed to be a weekend fling but I'm so hooked on your dick that I'm willing to further debase myself for a few more hours of your time," she said.

Braxton took a step back as if she'd slapped him. "So I'm wrong? You really just want the fuck?"

Carmen hung her head, ready to let the elevator take her back down to the lobby and away from his pending rejection. Instead, as the elevator slowed to their floor, Braxton pulled her snugly against him once more and guided her to the room he'd gotten for them.

"We're both hungry and tired. Let's not continue this conversation until after at least one of our needs is met," he said.

Braxton opened the hotel room door and Carmen couldn't help the surprised gasp that escaped her. Not only had he brought her to the fanciest hotel in town, he'd splurged for the honeymoon suite with all the trappings. The room was lit with candles, rose petals littered every surface and a candlelit dinner sat waiting in front of the large bank of windows with an amazing view of the Sowell River.

Whatever black cloud that had formed over things in the elevator evaporated as she took in the romantic set up. She escaped his grasp moving over to the windows to see the view.

"Oh my! I wish I had my camera," she gushed.

"I'll be sure to remind you to bring it up our next visit," Braxton chuckled.

Surprised, she turned to look at him.

"Braxton," she began but her words died in her throat as he lifted his shirt over his head.

"You wanted to fuck, Carmen. I'm here for as long as it's still good for the both of us," he said making a show of sliding out of his boots and jeans.

She swooned, leaning against the cool glass at her back to stave off the heat rising in her body as she watched him strip. He closed the distance between them and crowded her body with his.

"I don't know if you got the memo, but this is a clothing free establishment," he grinned down at her.

Yeah, whatever doubts she had in that elevator were definitely staying there, at least for the rest of the night.

"Oh dear, I was unaware," she stammered.

It wasn't hard to put on the act. Carmen was most definitely flustered.

"Well, it's a very strict code and failure to comply comes with its own punishment," he said.

"Punishment?"

She raised an eyebrow at that, but she didn't have to wait long to know what he had in store. He pushed the arms of her maxi dress off her shoulders and dragged them down her arms until the entire dress fell in a heap around her ankles. She hadn't put on a bra and her taut nipples were on full display for him.

"I really wanted to see how into the whole role-playing thing we could get, but *damn* you're beautiful, Carmen."

She blinked a few times as he just stood staring at her. "You've seen much more than this," she said.

Braxton shook his head. "Yeah, I've seen you naked. I've had my mouth and hands all over you but I wasn't really looking. Especially not like this."

His hot gaze trailing over her body was more intimate than any touch she'd ever experienced. She found her hand reaching up to play with her nipples, loving how dark his eyes got, how shallow his breathing became, as he watched her tease herself.

"Don't be shy, reach into those pretty panties of yours," he commanded, as he freed himself from his boxers and began stroking himself.

Carmen smiled, sliding her hand slowly from her nipple down her abdomen and into her panties as instructed. Her fingers slid effortlessly over her wet folds but she didn't dare touch her clit. Not until he told her to.

"Show me how wet you are."

She began to slide her underwear over her hips but he shook his head.

"If you take those off, our food will be refrigerator cold by the time we eat. Just your fingers, Carmen. Show me your fingers."

Before she showed him, she slid her middle finger deep inside of herself, exaggerating the movement so he knew exactly what she was doing before she pulled her hand free. She held up three shiny fingers before dropping all but the middle one and rubbing her essence on her tongue.

"You sure whatever dessert you planned will be as sweet as me?"

Braxton and his condom-clad erection closed the short distance between them faster than Carmen could blink. "No way in hell," he growled and snatched her underwear clean off.

With her bare ass and dripping wet pussy now exposed to the world he spun her around and entered her from behind. He fucked her mercilessly against the glass for all to see and when she was little more than a shuddering mass of sensation, he carried her over to the table and sat her wanton ass down in the chair across from his with a self-satisfied smirk.

Food. He needed to focus on the food in front of him, not the woman who so easily turned him into a sexual deviant. Braxton forced himself to saw into the room temperature steak and fill his mouth with beef instead of sweet Carmen pie. Taking his lead, Carmen did the same. The silence as they ate more deafening than her screams of pleasure just moments before.

Braxton hadn't realized just how bad he had it for Carmen, until he'd almost screwed things up in the elevator. He'd thought by playing up his playboy reputation it would help him control whatever it was that was happening between them. It hadn't. The moment she'd said all she wanted from him was the fucking, he'd felt like he'd been kicked in the gut.

All plans of this being the last night. Of him playing it safe had gone out the window. Now, he needed a new plan. One that allowed him to keep Carmen around long enough for her to get over Noah and maybe, just maybe, decide she too wanted more with him.

"You don't have to bring me back here for me to get pictures. I can maybe run down and grab my camera to snap a few, before heading to my friend's for the night," she said, breaking the silence.

Braxton stopped mid-chew to shoot her a glare. "If you think for one second you're staying anywhere but here tonight, you are out of your mind. Anyway, if you seriously can't wait until our next visit, I'll go with you to get your camera. Sowell City isn't the safest at night," he said.

"You worried about me being mugged, or do you subscribe to the fairytales about werewolves living amongst us," Carmen laughed.

Braxton sighed. Anyone who was in the Sowell Gate region for any length of time would have heard about the strange animal sightings and myths about shapeshifters. It was a running joke and part of the tourist draw for the area. Only, for Braxton and his family, it had become more than that, so her question wasn't the easiest for him to answer.

"You say you've been in Sowell City for two years? Spend a fair amount of time hiking the trails and you haven't had you're first strange encounter yet?"

"So, you are a believer! I never would have guessed," she said.

"I've lived in the Sowell Mountains my whole life. Generations of my family have. I don't believe in werewolves and shit like that, but I'd be lying if I said that there weren't spirits in the mountains. Things happen in this area that can't be explained by science and logic. Plus, this place is a magnet for crazies because of all the rumors, so it's better to be safe than sorry."

"Well, thank you for offering your protection. I'll consider your offer if you tell me more about this knowledge you have of the mountains. I've been on a few trails, mostly the popular well-travelled ones but I'd love the insider tips from a true local," she said.

Braxton smiled. "Now, that, I can do. Although my experience on the trails is more from the Edgewood side. People swear by the view of Sowell Gate from the Sowell City side but it's got nothing on the view from the private trails on my family estate," he said.

"Oh, so now not only do I get a repeat visit to this fancy hotel, but a private tour of your family estate? Why Braxton

Cross, I do believe that sounds shockingly like a date," she said with a fake southern accent.

"It could be if that's what you want. If not, we can call it a friendly hang," he offered.

Despite not being able to keep his dick in his pants, Braxton wasn't about to chase her away by pushing that he wanted more than she could offer him right now. Hell, he wasn't sure if it wasn't entirely his dick's obsession with her that was driving this need for more in the first place. It was better he kept both heads in check at this point. Play it cool.

"Nice segway into the friends with benefits chat, but sure. Let's hang out, fucking optional," she laughed.

"Fucking optional? Now who is lying to themselves," he muttered.

She laughed at his face and took another bite of steak. "Okay, new topic. How did you get into wood carving?"

Carmen listened as he told stories of sitting on the porch watching his grandfather whittle as a kid.

"He hated that he couldn't be up on the mountain anymore, but sitting in his rocking chair on the porch, molding the pieces of wood into whatever creation he wanted, that's what gave him joy in his final days. When I was too young to be on the mountain myself, I'd sit with him and watch. He was so meticulous, so careful with each movement of the knife," he said.

He remembered him trying to teach him. "I was too impatient to learn and never got past how to carve a nice pointy stick or a lopsided duck. When he passed, I regretted not learning more from him, so when my logging days were done, I picked it up again. I started small. As I got more confident and able to move around with more ease, I worked on bigger pieces. The rest is history," he said.

For once in her life, Carmen wished she were less curious. His story was touching and the stiff set of his shoulders and faraway look told her that it was merely the surface of how he'd gotten to where he was now. She would leave it alone, *should* leave it alone and preserve the lighter nature of their conversation, but one phrase he'd said begged for clarification.

"Move around more? What happened? Is that how you got your scar?"

The temperature in the room felt like it dropped ten degrees as Braxton refused to meet her gaze. She'd messed up again by asking him about the savage scarring that cut a jagged path across the entirety of his back. The dark cloud from the elevator had returned, only instead of hanging over them both, it was there in his eyes. Once glittering with amusement, now cloudy and distant.

After a moment of tense silence, he cleared his throat.

"Oh that? Yeah. Accidents happen, this one wasn't my first but," he paused for a moment before looking up at her. His eyes dark, with grief maybe, but then they warmed and a grin spread across his face, "Let's just say it taught me not to take life for granted. Right now, that means it's time for dessert."

It was obvious that he was deflecting and trying to lighten the mood but Carmen was not protesting as he pulled her out of the chair and lifted her onto the table. She gasped as he dove face first between her legs like a mad man possessed.

When he woke up to an empty bed, Braxton panicked. Jumping up he searched the room for a note but there was none. He was just shoving himself into his clothes to go hunt her down when the hotel room door opened and Carmen came in with two large coffees and something sweet-smelling in a bag from Flower Café.

"Hey! I thought you'd be sleep for a bit longer," she said standing on her tiptoes to press a kiss to his cheek.

"You should have left a note; I thought you'd disappeared on me again," he said sinking into a nearby chair.

She frowned before sliding into his lap.

"I'm sorry. I know that this is new and different for both of us. I promise I won't just up and leave you. It's not really my style anyway. Besides, maybe you were hoping I ghosted you again. We've had some intense few days but I know about the Wild Cross Brothers. You told me your usual MO yourself. Maybe I should be concerned you'll be the one to ghost me."

Braxton kissed her again, rubbing her ass with his palm. "Shit, Carmen. I have a reputation sure, but damn if you ain't the woman with the power to tame my ass."

Carmen laughed. "Hold on, lumberjack. As flattering as that is, and as amazing as our time has been, we need to be realistic about this friends-with-benefits thing, or whatever it is," she said sliding out of his lap and into the chair across from him.

She handed him a coffee and set a pastry in front of him. Not what he would consider a real breakfast but he wasn't about to complain and scare her off before he had a chance to plead his case with her.

Carmen had meant to make a run for it. Every cell in her brain told her to run far away from Braxton Cross and his magic hardwood but then she'd seen the outer suite. The remnants of their meal reminded her of the sweet way he let her ramble about her love of photography, and gave her tips on hiking trails on the other side of the mountain. Of course, he also offered to join her and show them to her himself. And then, he'd opened up to her about his grandfather and how he found his love for woodworking. That glimpse at the real Braxton had convinced her to make a little effort of her own, to show that she was willing to pursue whatever was blossoming between them.

So, she'd headed out to get them breakfast and looked up the accident. He hadn't wanted to tell her about it, but surely something that big had made the news. She read the article about it while she waited for their breakfast. The harrowing reporting of the logging accident that ended not just Braxton's logging career, but his uncle's life, had her heart aching. So yeah, instead of running away, she was running to be first in line when it came to the affections of one Braxton Cross.

He polished off his pastry in one massive bite and chugged down his coffee before sitting back and eyeing her in a way that had her squirming in her chair.

"Talking," she reminded him.

He smirked at her. "I have to make the drive back to Edgewood today. I have work and I'm sure you have things to do too."

She nodded in agreement, still watching him watch her as she took a dainty bite of her chocolate croissant. "I have a portrait session at noon and photos to edit from previous shoots," she said.

"So you'll give me your number, and I'll call you tonight before bed; make sure you're tucked in well and good," he said.

"I'm going to assume you mean phone sex, but I'll be on the couch at my friend's place, not the most private of settings for that kind of fun," she said trying not to sound disappointed.

"We'll figure it out. Either way, come Friday I'll make my way back over the mountain to spend the weekend with you again."

"You don't have to do that," she sighed.

He leaned closer and took her hand in his. "Carmen, I'm doing my best to try and give you the space to get over that asshat, but I'm going to be one hundred percent honest with you right now. I have already claimed your body as mine and as long as we have this arrangement in the works, I expect us to act accordingly," he said. He kissed her palm before letting her go. "Now eat your food so I can fuck you and get you a real meal before you have to start your day."

With that he disappeared into the bedroom and a few seconds later she heard the shower running. Carmen sat in stunned silence, letting his words truly sink in. Her flight instinct reared its ugly head again, but she shoved it down with the rest of her croissant and washed it away with the remainder of her coffee. What she needed was a break from all things men until she got her shit together, but if Braxton kept up this wicked sweet and sexy thing, she'd be a goner for sure.

CHAPTER 5

Braxton spent the entire drive home planning his great seduction of Carmen Quinn. He knew she wasn't ready. Hell, Braxton wasn't sure he was doing either of them a favor by pursuing whatever this thing was between them. All he knew was that he wanted more of Carmen, like he'd never wanted more of any woman he'd ever been with. So, he created a plan he hoped had enough built-in safe-outs, in case things went south. He even had a mental checklist by the time he pulled through the gates of his family estate.

Step 1 – Wine & Dine – show her that he had some class and could be romantic.

Step 2 – Nature's Way – Explore their shared love of nature and help her get some amazing photographs to add to her portfolio, show her that he cared about her work.

Step 3 – Family & Friends – he would need to win over the people close to her, show her that he wasn't going to treat her the way Noah had, and ostracize her from those closest to her.

Step 4 – Rock her world – he'd already done this step, but he had every intention of continuing their amazing sexual relationship throughout the courtship, as long as she was okay with it.

He ran the checklist over and over as he carried her photographs from his truck into his cabin. He'd forgotten they were in the cab, otherwise he would have dropped them with her at her studio before hitting the road. He'd called her on the drive up to let her know he had them and she told him he could bring them by that weekend. With that settled, he changed into his work clothes and made his way out to his workshop. He had three major orders to finish mocking up before the end of the week. Losing more than half the day meant he'd have to work late to make up the time.

"You're getting a late start," Hunter said leaning against Braxton's work bench.

Braxton looked up at his cousin and scowled.

"Yep, so unless you have something important to say, scram," he said.

Hunter laughed. "Fine, but your Ma wants us all at dinner tonight. She sent me to remind you not to be late."

Braxton sighed. He knew his mother and the rest of the family would all have questions about Carmen, but he'd hoped to get at least the night to come up with a good explanation for his behavior that wouldn't have his mother seeing another wedding on the horizon. Carmen was amazing. He couldn't discount the possibility of her being the one, but right now was not the time to be making those kinds of insinuations. Especially in front of his mother.

"I'll be there," Braxton grumbled.

"Good, looking forward to it," Hunter said, before walking away.

With Hunter out of his hair, he pulled out his phone and made a call he didn't want to make, but knew he had to. With Bechet out of town, his only other contact with the people of Corinthian was Margo Buchanan, the only person Bechet trusted to handle the contracts for their still growing offshoot of the family company.

"Braxton! You've been a naughty boy," she teased as soon as she answered.

"So you've heard," he said.

"Oh, a lot of people heard you and your mystery girl. Was she really dressed like Carmen San Diego? I mean, gosh that was one of my fantasies as a kid. Anyway, the owners were pissed but I managed to calm them down. You already paid for the damage to the room," she said.

"Yeah, about that little detail. I definitely paid more than that crappy plywood shit was worth. Any chance you could smooth talk them into letting us handle their economy rooms, as well as their luxury ones?"

"Brax, doll, you know I already got you covered. Now obviously the budget isn't exactly desirable and I had to play it humble since you literally fucked us into this deal," she said.

"I got it, alright. I screwed up but did they go for it?" he asked.

"Yeah, they did. They want affordable mocks by the end of the month. Think you can handle that, with everything else you have on your plate?"

"Yeah, I just need to wrap up a few solo customs and then I'll tackle this project. Send me the specs?"

"Already done, oh, and Brax... I'm sure Bechet wouldn't have minded you breaking shit at K Hotel instead of one of our valued clients," Margo said.

He rolled his eyes at her joke. "Yeah yeah. Anyway, I see the specs in my email, I'll send pics when I'm done."

He hung up the phone before she could say anything more to try to riled him up. With that business out of the way, he could get back to what he actually enjoyed.

Carmen smiled as four-year-old Marissa Carter insisted on standing on one leg for her birthday photos. Marissa had firmly cemented her spot as Carmen's favorite client the moment they'd met. Baby Marissa had given Carmen the cutest little baby smile and gripped her pinky tight. The interaction had set the tone for all of their photoshoots. Carmen was the only photographer the little girl's parents trusted to handle the her portraits ever since.

This year, however, was a little more difficult as Marissa had grown into voicing her own opinion about things. She'd wanted a ballerina shoot but her parents insisted she continue the tradition of a princess theme. The pose was a compromise, but Carmen knew that Margaret Carter was not happy with her child. Carmen snapped a few of this particular pose before getting the entire family in to do a more serious portrait.

Despite the pretentious airs the family liked to put on, the Carters were a loving, middle-class family. They came in every year for holiday photos and Marissa's birthday photos. In fact, the Carters had been her first repeat customers back when she'd worked out of the garage at Noah's condo. She finished up their shoot and gave the Carters a sneak peek at a few of the better shots.

"I'll give you a call when I'm done editing," she promised as she led them to the front door.

"Thanks again Carmen, and do tell Noah we say hello," Margaret said.

For a moment, Carmen's easy smile faltered but luckily the family was already out the door. The Carters wouldn't be the last to bring up Noah with her. Hell, it had barely been twenty-four hours since Noah had been notified of the end of their relationship. She had no idea how to even address the breakup with the few people she still interacted with, who knew them as a couple. As if the universe had sensed her need to not be alone at the moment, Imena, Scarlett, and Amayah came walking in.

"You're done with shooting for the day, right? A talk needs to be had young lady," Amayah said.

She tried to divert that attention because with all of it focused on her, it was intense. And not in the fun way that she'd felt with Braxton. "Amayah shouldn't you be at work? Imena, who's watching the boutique while you're over here? And Scar don't you have a class right now?"

The three women glared at Carmen, and she begrudgingly let them into her studio. They grabbed the few folding chairs that acted as Carmen's studio seating and waited.

"Noah cheated on me. I went to his hotel. A woman answered the door wearing the shirt I bought him for Christmas," Carmen said.

"That rat bastard! Tell me you whooped his ass, her ass, made a whole fucking scene!" Scarlett said.

"You know she didn't. I'm sorry you had to experience that," Amayah said.

"Ugh can we skip all the ways Noah is a useless asshole and get to the good stuff. I want to know about Carmen's new lover," Imena said.

"He's not my anything, we had a fun weekend," Carmen shrugged.

"Lies. I heard about the fight you and Noah had, and how he stepped in at the airport. I know people who work there," Imena said.

Carmen rolled her eyes because Imena knew everyone, period. She never met a stranger she couldn't immediately read and charm. At least as far as Carmen knew.

"He didn't follow me from Mulberry or anything creepy like that. He just happens to live in the same area. He helped me out with a few things and I finished up our weekend rendezvous last night," Carmen admitted.

"Name please," Scarlett said.

Carmen rolled her eyes. Was it really so bad that she wanted to keep this to herself a bit longer? To see if Braxton was even worth mentioning to her small group of friends? Honestly, it didn't matter. Imena already knew who her mystery fling was. As if all the clues weren't already there, Imena's friend had no doubt seen exactly who had come to her rescue and told Imena all about it. The Cross family and more specifically this latest generation of Cross men were the closest to hometown celebrities as Sowell City got, aside from some K pop star that was rumored to also be from the area.

"Braxton, his name is Braxton."

"Braxton Cross! You're fucking Braxton Break Your Bed and Back, second in the line of Cross your heart, you don't catch feelings!" Scarlett shrieked.

Carmen grimaced. "Oh god, he's actually called that?" she said.

"Not to his face, but in the circle of women who dare speak of their encounters with him and his brothers, yeah," Scarlett said.

"Are you one of them?" Carmen couldn't help but ask. Her gut twisted in knots as she waited for Scarlett to answer.

"No, I don't fuck where I eat. I'm one of the investors for Cross Furniture, but to be clear if I ever did, it would have been with Bechet; he's more my style, but he's already spoken for. Anyway, good for you honey. If you were looking for a proper fuck buddy to help you get over Noah's ass, then you picked a good one."

Carmen wanted to be okay with what Scarlett admitted to her, but it still left her all twisted up inside. She should be okay with a fuck buddy. She didn't want a relationship right now, but what Scarlett was implying – and what she already knew about Braxton's MO – didn't exactly line up with her experience with him. Sure, he'd been a beast in bed, but he'd also given her a glimpse of his softer side. But Carmen couldn't be sure of her judgment when it came to men. Noah was a prime example of her failure to recognize red flags, even as they were being waved right in front of her eyes.

"You okay, Carmen?" Amayah asked, concern clear on her face.

"Excuse me," Carmen said and rushed off to the small restroom in the back corner, before she got sick all over her studio floor.

"Shit! Carmen, I'm sorry I brought it up. Don't mind me, you know I'm jaded, a good time kind of girl," Scarlett said from outside the bathroom door.

"It's not, it's okay. I think I'm just overwhelmed with everything that's going on. I get sick when I'm stressed," Carmen said when she emerged from the bathroom.

Imena handed her a hot cup of tea that she'd probably brought over from the Sowell Sisters Office next door. Carmen accepted it and took a sip. She'd thought that would be the end of the discussion, that once she showed them she was okay, they would go back to their respective jobs and not bring it up again until their standing girls' night. She was wrong. Instead, while Imena and Scarlett tended to Carmen, Amayah had apparently rounded up the rest of the Sowell Sisters.

Vega, Artemis, and Savita were all crowded into her small studio space.

"What's going on?"

"We are all taking the day off for a little time in nature," Amayah said.

Twenty minutes later, the group of women were hiking one of the more casual trails along the bottom of the Sowell Gate Mountains. Carmen didn't want to admit it, but this was exactly what she needed. Time away from it all, in nature, hanging out with women around her age, chatting about anything and everything except men.

"We should do more outdoor weddings. I'm tired of planning stuffy hotel ballroom affairs," Savita said.

"Girl, don't complain about what's keeping the lights on. I love the good outdoors as much as you do but we both know the logistics of it would be a nightmare," Artemis said.

"Also, getting permission to hold large gatherings up here would be a stretch. Although, the social media buzz, if we could finagle an agreement, would be amazing," Vega said.

"Sustainable weddings are totally a thing. I went to one where instead of throwing rice they had the wedding party clean the beach before the ceremony," Scarlett said.

"Eww, I'd have respectfully declined that invitation," Amayah shuddered.

"What, you not for the environment?" Carmen teased.

"It's not that. Just do it because you want to, in the appropriate beach cleaning clothing. Like, who wants to drop hundreds on a dress to go pick up garbage? Not to mention I'm sure they did it for social media and probably only cleaned before and not after the ceremony," Amayah said.

Imena laughed.

"And I thought Artemis was the cynic of the group," Vega said.

"I'm not a cynic. I just know the type of people Scarlett hung out with before she was so very lucky to find us," Amayah said.

"I feel like I should be offended right now," Scarlett said.

"Don't be, Amayah is just being snippy because of work stuff," Imena said.

"What did those assholes do now?" Carmen asked.

"Oh, it's just the usual office boys club stuff," Amayah said.

"Oh." Carmen made a face, especially knowing that the boys club included Noah.

Carmen had first met Amayah at a work event with Noah. She'd been nice and they had clicked over their love of Gen Ursa novels. Noah hadn't been thrilled with their friendship, now that Carmen thought about it. If she hadn't ignored his disapproving comments about the friendship, where would she be now? Probably still under Noah's thrall. Miserable with no accomplishments to show for herself. He'd texted her that morning, but she had yet to read the message. She just wasn't willing to deal with him yet, if at all.

"Don't do that," Imena said.

"Don't do what?" Vega stopped walking to get in on the conversation.

"She's thinking about her ex," Imena said.

"Right, he works with you right?" Artemis asked Amayah.

"Unfortunately," Amayah said.

"He hasn't said anything to you, has he?" Carmen bit her lip.

Amayah shook her head. "No, you know Noah and I were never really on casual speaking terms. Imena, why did you even bring it up? We are supposed to be destressing on this hike and now Carmen looks like she's about to cry," Amayah huffed.

"I'm not going to cry. It's just all still fresh," Carmen said.

"Right, but not as fresh as that hickey on your neck," Scarlett said and poked Carmen just behind her ear.

The reminder of her time with Braxton did the trick to pull her out of her Noah-induced funk. Now instead of feeling on the verge of rage tears, she patted her cheeks as heat made them rosy. Was Braxton working on another masterpiece? Meeting virtually with clients to discuss the nitty-gritty of contracts? No, the picture of him with his shirt off, sweating over a thick slab of wood as he honed it into a work of art was exactly what he was doing as far as she was concerned.

"Destressing and avoiding all male-related subjects. Focus," Artemis snapped.

"Right, look at how thick this tree trunk is, and doesn't that rock formation have the most lickable bulbous shape at the tip? Almost like a scoop of ice cream," Scarlett gushed.

They all turned to glare at her and she laughed before skipping further down the trail. Carmen shook her head to clear out the picture of something else tall, thick, and with a bulbous-headed rock formation.

Damn you, Scarlett.

It took another half mile to get Carmen's head off Braxton and what he might be doing with his day. When they stopped for a break at one of the scenic spots overlooking Sowell City, Carmen pulled out her camera and started snapping away. She'd taken pictures here a few times before, but this time she wasn't just taking pictures of the greenery. Her focus was on the group of women who'd rallied around her in her time of need.

Scarlett the party girl, as she bent to retie her custom pink hiking boots. Amayah, as she did an impression of a gazelle leaping down the trail. Imena and Savita sitting cross legged on a boulder meditating. Artemis looking grumpy and stoic as she scanned the tree line ahead of them. Her picture came out with a slight green glow around her, probably a trick of the sunlight filtering through the trees that had yet to turn with the weather. Then there was Vega with her face turned longingly up to the sky, arms spread out as if she wished nothing more than to be soaring up in the clouds, not a care in the world.

Carmen could totally relate to that sentiment. The need to soar above all of her worries; that's why she was here now. To get away from it all.

After the hike, they all went to Scarlett's favorite restaurant for dinner. Sowell Garden, a local institution that, despite her years in the city, Carmen had never tried before. The chef himself came out to greet them, an Asian-American man that clearly had Scarlett's undivided attention. Carmen made a note to ask Scarlett about that later. For now, she enjoyed her first taste of Korean fusion cuisine, and the companionship of the women around her.

"Oh, Carmen, I'm going to be a little late tonight but I made you a copy of the key to my place," Imena said handing her the key.

"Thank you. I hope I don't have to couch surf for long. It's just going to be rough finding a decent rental with the college in session and hiking season," she said.

"No worries, I'll see you later, okay?" Imena trotted off before Carmen could say anything more.

"That girl gets flightier every day," Artemis grumbled.

"Hey! No grumbling behind her back, Art. Anyway, I've got to get going if I'm going to make it to Sullah before dark," Vega said.

"Yarrow is waiting up for me but Carmen, feel free to call me if you need anything," Amayah said.

"Drive safe," Carmen said.

That left Carmen and Scarlett at the table alone. Savita had left earlier to get more work done before the end of the day.

"So, what's with you and Chef Kim?" Carmen asked.

"Nothing," Scarlett sighed longingly as she stared at the doors to the kitchen.

"I wouldn't exactly call this nothing," Carmen mimicking Scarlett's wistful look.

Scarlett made a face before sipping her water. "So, I'm guessing the embargo on man talk has been lifted," she muttered.

"Scar, just spill," Carmen said.

"Okay, so I have a crush, like a huge one, and for once the man I'm after wants jack all to do with me," she huffed.

Carmen chuckled. "A man immune to your stunning looks and sparkling personality? That's definitely a first. You sure he's single?"

Scarlett bit her lip. "Yep, he spends all his time at work or with his family. Doesn't give me the time of day unless I'm here as a customer," she said.

"Wow, it's not like you to be this hung up on someone who doesn't want you. You sure you aren't like punishing yourself because of what happened with Matty?"

Scarlett tensed up at the mention of her beloved dog, who'd been missing for months before Amayah found him and her dog Matilda in the mountains.

"Maybe? I don't know. Ugh, let me cover the bill and then we can go," she said and stood before Carmen could say anything more.

The hostess didn't seem shocked that Scarlett went to her to pay instead of waiting for the bill to come to them. The two women left the restaurant, stopping to hug each other before going their separate ways.

Imena's place was homey in that hipster witch kind of way. Tapestries, candles, an altar in the corner of the living room. Carmen didn't believe in magic or any of that metaphysical stuff, but Imena was good people and she hadn't gotten a bad vibe off the woman in the year that she'd known her, so she didn't mind. Carmen cleaned up and changed into her pajamas before grabbing her sleeping bag and settling onto the couch. She deleted Noah's texts without reading them before she sent a quick text to Braxton saying she was headed to bed. After ten minutes, and no reply, she closed her eyes and drifted off to sleep.

The tension at the Cross family dinner table was thicker than the mountain of mashed potatoes on Braxton's plate. His mother had yet to question him about Carmen, but only because Baron had just dropped a fucking bomb on the whole family.

"That bitch wants more money, saying I caused her severe emotional distress that doesn't allow her to work!" Baron snapped in the middle of serving himself another helping of baked ham.

He'd been stewing all night. It had only been a matter of time before he blew, but it had still come as a shock to everyone.

"Keep your voice down, shouting is not going to solve your problem," their mom hissed.

"Boy, you need to handle this ex-wife of yours, before I get the cousins to handle her the old-fashioned way," Wilhelm Cross said.

His green eyes sparkling, and his cheeks ruddy and quaking in anger. By cousins, he didn't mean Hunter, who had basically lived with them his entire life, but the less talked about Crosses. The ones that only crawled out of their tinfoil-covered cabins to stock up on ammo and rile shit up. If Wilhelm was willing to call in the less reputable part of the Cross family tree, things were really getting to the old man. Wilhelm had dealt with his own family's racism when he'd married Melinda Westmoore, but they hadn't treated him or his brothers any differently because they were half Black.

They were Crosses by blood, and family loyalty meant more than their personal prejudices, even if they didn't always understand the cultural differences of growing up half Black in a mostly white and mostly racist area. Didn't make them the best family, but even they had given Baron the side eye for marrying his soon-to-be ex-wife.

They'd known more about Christine and her family than Baron had, and none of them had been surprised when the truth about her long-term affair came out and ended their already fucked up union. Now she was making Baron's life a living hell by dragging out the proceedings of their divorce, and causing unnecessary drama like showing up to Bechet's wedding knowing damn well she wasn't invited. Thank God for prenups, or his older brother wouldn't have a chance.

"I'll handle it. I just want you to know, in case she tries to use you all to strengthen her case," Baron said.

"You don't have anything to worry about from me," Braxton said.

"I've been better about keeping my exploits under wraps lately, so I don't think that will be a problem," Hunter said.

"Baron, are you sure you are going to be okay? I know Elias is helping with this, but is anything else we can do?" their mother asked.

"I'm fine, it will all be fine. I can't wait until I never have to see that woman again," he said.

Wilhelm took a big swig from his whiskey glass and settled a glare on his sons. Braxton held his breath for whatever edict his father was about to pass down.

"Look, I messed up, forcing Baron to do what was right by that girl all those years ago. You all better take this as the lesson it is and don't go knocking up any hussies and tarnishing the Cross name," he said.

Hunter rolled his eyes and Braxton took a sip from his own whiskey glass.

"Pa, we learned that lesson when Christine first came up pregnant," Hunter said.

"Accidents happen," Melinda snorted.

Wilhelm glared at his wife. That was the closest his mother had ever come to confirming that Baron hadn't been born early like their parents claimed. Not like anyone believed it, with how big Baron was in his infant pictures. All the Cross boys had been born big but not that big. Melinda just shrugged and turned her gaze on Braxton.

"Speaking of female friends, Braxton, I believe, has some explaining to do," she said.

He'd known this was coming but he still hadn't been prepared. He looked to his brother for a little help, but Baron was all too happy to shift the focus from his failed marriage to him.

"Yes, the girl at the airport. How did your friend get settled?" Baron said, an amused glint in his eye.

"I met Carmen at the hotel bar after Bechet's wedding. She looked like she needed a friend so I bought her a drink. When I saw her at the airport, I knew she was in a bad spot and figured I could help her out. I helped her move her things from her ex's place to a friend's. Crashed at a hotel for the night and came home. That's all there is to it."

"Boy, I hope you never have to lie for business reasons, 'cos you can't fib for shit," Wilhelm cursed.

"Yeah, cuz. We heard exactly what you said to her ex-boyfriend. Not to mention that kiss," Hunter piped up.

"Honey, it's okay to have feelings for a girl. Just be careful this one doesn't break your heart," Melinda said.

Baron sat there shaking his head. "If you really like this girl, then let her go. You won't stand a chance as the rebound guy," he said.

Braxton finished his whiskey. "Y'all are jumpin the gun here. Like I said, Carmen and I are just friends. I'm allowed to have female friends, aren't I?"

"Sure cuz, whatever you say." Hunter laughed.

Most of the time Braxton loved that his family was so close. Now was not one of those times. Luckily, talk turned to Bechet's wedding again, and once dinner was over Braxton rushed back to his cabin to check his phone. It was late and he'd missed a text from Carmen by about an hour. It was too late to hope she'd be awake, but he didn't want her thinking he didn't care so he shot her a text back before getting himself ready for bed.

The conversation with his family had him second-guessing his seduction plans for Carmen. He wanted her sure, but at what cost? How far was he willing to stick his neck out on the off chance that Carmen might want to be with him? Then there was the question of how long and to what end? Carmen didn't strike him as the casual sex kind of girl, despite the weekend they'd shared. She was an all-or-nothing type for sure, but if she wasn't ready to give her all, why should he force the issue? Did he even want her all?

A sharp ache hit his chest as he thought about it. He was digging too deep here. He closed his eyes, focusing on the montage of the many ways he'd had her that weekend. It wasn't long before he was fisting his own cock but despite getting off, he wasn't nearly satisfied. This was going to be a long four days.

CHAPTER 6

Carmen was just finishing her consultation with the Weavers for their son's senior photos when none other than Braxton came waltzing into her studio. In his hands were the portraits he'd accidentally left in his truck the weekend before. He nodded at the Weavers as he carefully propped them against the wall.

"I really look forward to the shoot next week," Carmen said, hoping to stop the Weavers' open gawking.

Mr. Weaver turned back to Carmen, a curious glint in his eyes but at least he had the decency to gather up his family.

"Right, we shall see you next week," Mr. Weaver said, and ushered them out the door.

Braxton nodded at them again as they left, his massive frame making her already small waiting area look even tinier.

"What are you doing here? I thought we were meeting at the hotel," Carmen said.

Braxton smirked and pulled her into his arms before kissing her. "I figured it was easier for me to drop these here and I couldn't wait to see you," he said.

"That horny, huh?" she laughed.

"I am definitely hard right now, but no. I actually just needed to see you," he said.

The warm fluttering in her stomach caught her off guard. Not only had he been thoughtful enough to return her photographs to her at her studio, but he needed to see her? Like just be in her presence see her? If Braxton took any more pages out of her favorite romance novels, she was surely in trouble. Carmen pulled out of his grasp.

"Give me a second to close up shop and I can meet you at the hotel," she said.

She didn't want to address the something more that she felt happening between them. She'd only just gotten okay with the overwhelming desire to be with him sexually. Other than Monday, he'd called her every night to tell her all the ways he wanted to fuck her that weekend, and she was more than ready for everything he had in store for her. At least sexually, not emotionally. Emotionally, she had decided she was cutting herself off.

Especially because for every sweet and sexy text Braxton sent her, Noah had sent an angry one. She decided to stop ignoring his texts and finally deal with him head on. At first, he'd tried to win her back. She'd been prepared for that. No amount of sweet talking would change what she'd seen or what she'd been feeling during the last few years of their on and off again relationship.

When he realized she wasn't backing down, that's when the blaming started. She had made him look bad at the airport; she would regret moving out when she fell flat on her face without his support. Then he'd called her all sorts of names and threatened to sue for damages for what she and Braxton had done to his bed. She'd hung up on him, blocked his number and made a note to send a cashier's check to cover the cost of a new bed. His bed hadn't been that expensive but it still stung, further depleting her new apartment fund. She probably should have blocked him the night she caught him cheating.

Catching Noah had been a wake up call for her. A slap to the face, a kick in the gut. She was still pissed about the situation; not just because of Noah, but also for being so blinded by her feelings she hadn't seen the walls closing in around her. He'd thoroughly trapped her with lies so paper-thin she should have seen through them all, but she hadn't. Until she could trust her judgment again, sex was all she would allow herself. Even that would be off the table if it weren't for the fact that Braxton was such a fucking meal.

"Actually, I was hoping to take you out to dinner first," Braxton said.

"Sure, we can grab some takeout on the way," Carmen said, keeping an even smile as she grabbed her purse.

Braxton stopped her at the door and leveled her with a serious look. "Are you running from me, Carmen?"

She groaned and looked away from him. "I'm not running. I just don't want to get confused about what's going on between us. I know your reputation and hell, in this case, I welcome it, but I also know I easily get caught up in my emotions and I can't afford another disappointment," she admitted.

"I know what you've heard, and what I've said out my own damn mouth but I don't care about that. I just care that you don't go overthinking the plain and simple truth. We both like each other. So, let's enjoy that. We can talk and be friends and trash hotel rooms with our fucking and do whatever makes us feel good, for as long as it feels good to do it," he said.

"Why are you like this?"

"Like what?"

"Like some crass but sweet, romance novel type, knight in shining armor," Carmen said.

Braxton made a face before bursting into laughter. "Why don't you hold off on that assessment until you get to know me a little better, alright? Starting with a proper fucking dinner date."

Braxton couldn't get Carmen's words out of his head. She thought he, of all people, was sweet. Not just that, but a romantic savior type. He'd been lying if he said he didn't kind of enjoy that thought, even knowing his past when it came to women. The problem was that that wasn't him. Braxton wasn't sweet, or a knight, and his savior attitude had nothing to do with him being a good Samaritan and everything to do with him wanting unfettered access to her body.

He was not a romance novel character. At least not the kind he'd read once in high school out of curiosity. He'd seen a few of the girls in school reading the tiny little things with red covers and fancy gold script you could find at the grocery store. He'd seen them tear the cover off or hide them in larger more appropriate books to read during school and even at church.

So yeah, he'd picked one up one day and while he could see the appeal, the male characters' actions just never rang true to him. When a woman said no you left them alone. If you really loved a woman, you wouldn't let a stupid misunderstanding keep you apart for years, and Braxton was too careful to have any secret baby lying around somewhere. That shit made for some wild stories but wasn't real life. It was those novels that made him see the best policy with women was to be upfront with them from the start. No sugar coating, no teasing, just cold hard facts about where you stood. They could take it or leave it.

"You're not eating," Carmen said, breaking into his thoughts.

He looked down at his plate and sure enough, he hadn't even cut into his steak let alone made a dent in his stuffed baked potato.

"Sorry, I was just thinking," he said.

"About what?"

He sliced off a piece of steak and shoved it in his mouth. "You," he said around the hunk of meat.

Braxton did have better manners, but he was trying to prove a point here about not being a romance novel type. Carmen smiled and took a bite out of her blue cheese burger. He didn't begrudge a woman with an appetite, but blue cheese was disgusting. Something Carmen knew he didn't like after they'd ordered wings that first weekend and they'd brought all blue cheese dressing instead of all ranch like he'd asked. It seemed he wasn't the only one trying to make this less than what it was.

They ate mostly in silence. Him, making it a point to smack on his food, her savoring every bite of her blue cheese monstrosity but then the amused look in her eyes shifted to one of shock then anger. Braxton followed her gaze and cursed. Her asshole ex had just been seated right in her line of sight with a few other men dressed in suits. Braxton could have written it off as a coincidence if the man didn't look directly at them and narrow his eyes.

Braxton smiled at the man and waved. The move garnered the attention of the other man's party. It was clear that they had questions for Carmen's ex about why she was there with someone else. That was almost enough for Braxton to let the man be, even as his palms itched with the urge to walk over and plant his fist in the man's face just on principle.

Braxton turned back to Carmen who was chugging her beer and glaring at her ex over the bottle. He reached over and took it from her, finishing off the beer for her.

"Don't let him see that he's getting to you," he snapped.

She glared at him before her gaze dropped to her plate. He could see tears brimming in her eyes and that was not gonna happen on his watch. He took her hand in his, bringing it to his lips. He pressed a soft kiss across her knuckles.

"I'm sorry for my tone, I just don't like seeing you upset," he said.

"It's not really because of Noah. I mean, yeah, he's an asshole and I deserve better. Just every time I see him, I'm reminded that I allowed it to happen. It's my fault I stuck around and let him control certain aspects of my life, even knowing deep down that he wasn't the one for me," Carmen said.

"Damn straight he wasn't. You shouldn't be so hard on yourself. It may have taken you longer than you would have liked to end things with him, but you did. Besides, if you had kicked him to the curb sooner, would you have ended up here with me? Would we have been able to have all that fun wrecking that bedroom last week? Some things happen the way they do for a reason," Braxton said.

"As fun as that was, I forked over half my new apartment fund to cover the damages so he wouldn't come after us both," Carmen groaned.

Braxton let go of her hand while he reined in the instant rage he felt that she had even bothered to do such a thing.

"How much? I'll repay you."

Carmen shook her head. "Don't worry about it. In the long run it's nothing if he'll leave me alone for good."

"It's not nothing," Braxton said and stood from the table.

He marched over to where Noah sat with his buddies. The table fell silent as he approached, all eyes turned to him wide with a mixture of shock, curiosity and fear.

"Mr. Cross, to what do I owe this pleasure?" Noah said, a smirk on his face.

The man was clearly trying to save face. Braxton wasn't about to have any of that.

"This isn't about to be some friendly chat. I'm only going to say this once. You fucked up by cheating on Carmen and she's done with you. So, if you continue to harass her – in person or otherwise – it won't be the cops at your door but me. Understand?"

Noah was white as a ghost after Braxton's not so veiled threat. Braxton couldn't even care less that there were witnesses to it either. All he cared about was that Carmen didn't have to deal with anything else when it came to Noah. She'd already gone through more than enough.

"I...I don't know what lies..." Noah didn't get to finish his sentence before Braxton grabbed him by the collar and yanked him out of the booth.

Braxton's limited patience with the man had already worn out. He was just about to put his fist through the man's face when Carmen intervened. "Braxton, that's enough!"

He looked over his shoulder and his anger deflated almost immediately. She looked shocked and embarrassed; he hated that this time he was the cause of those emotions. He tossed Noah back toward his booth before getting out his wallet and dropping a couple bills on the table.

"Y'all should take your meals to go," he hissed before turning back to Carmen.

She was already facing away from him and headed back to their table. Braxton followed without looking back, but he could hear the waitress asking the men if they wanted their order to go. Hell, he wouldn't be surprised if he and Carmen were asked to leave as well. Then again, he was a Cross, and sometimes that meant he got away with things that others wouldn't.

It seemed this time was another one of those cases. When the waitress stopped by it was only to offer them refills on their drinks and to let them know that desert had been comped. Carmen, however, wasn't about to let him off the hook so easy.

"I can't believe you did that!"

"You just told me he was harassing you for money. I was about to kick his ass for being in your presence, and you expected me not to do anything after that?"

"I didn't tell you for you to go all agro on him. Hell, I didn't mean to tell you at all. Noah isn't your problem. He's mine."

"Noah's not your problem anymore. Hasn't been from the moment you climbed on my dick."

Carmen rolled her eyes. "I don't get you, Braxton. At least not in the context of a real-life person. Your actions make perfect sense for a romantic hero. You jumping in to save the damsel in distress."

"Here you go again with the romance hero nonsense. First, you are no damsel in distress. I haven't known you very long, but I know enough to see that you can handle your own shit. You don't need me to swoop in and save you. That doesn't stop me from wanting to though, even if it's only to keep you in my bed. It might not make sense to you, but it makes all the sense in the world to me."

"Technically, I haven't been in your bed," Carmen quipped.

Braxton smiled and brushed his finger along her wrist. Her lips parted in a small gasp. "If I paid for it, it's my bed. Which is why I'm going to repay you whatever you shelled out to that asshole. Don't get me wrong, I don't regret what we did – hell, I thoroughly enjoyed myself – but it don't sit right with me, having you in another man's bed."

"I'll think about it," Carmen said pulling her arm away.

Braxton could see this line of conversation would end up with him talking himself out of bed with Carmen this weekend so he changed topics.

"I saw the pictures you posted from your hike earlier this week. I didn't know you knew Scarlett King," he said.

Carmen looked up, confusion in her eyes. "You follow me on social media?"

"I looked you up, to see more of your photography work."

"Oh, okay. Anyway, yes, Scarlett and I are friends."

"Funny, you two don't seem like you'd have much in common. Scarlett always seemed the shallow party girl type. Aside from her investing savvy of course," he said.

"Party girl most definitely, shallow not at all. I honestly think she plays that bit up to throw people off, but she's really a sweetheart once you get to know her," Carmen said.

He waited for the other shoe to drop. For Carmen to make a fuss about their shared acquaintance. To be fair, Scarlett King was a little more than just an acquaintance, she was arguably a friend of the family, even if she was banned from all gatherings hosted or attended by his mother. He didn't know the full story about that since he'd been away when the infamous party fiasco occurred, but it had to be bad for Scarlett to not even be invited to Bechet's wedding.

"You not going to ask me how I know her?"

Carmen shook her head. "She's already assured me your relationship is all business."

Braxton smiled. "Were you worried it wasn't?"

Carmen picked up her burger and took another huge bite, obviously avoiding the answer to that question. Braxton picked his fork back up and started to eat again, this time with the manners he was raised on. His annoyance at her romance hero nonsense was replaced with a sick sort of pride that she'd shown even the slightest hint of being jealous and territorial over him. They kept their conversation light as they ate. Despite his best efforts, he hated that her gaze still tracked over his shoulder to the table that had once seated her ex. Braxton couldn't even enjoy his meal knowing that his company still wasn't enough to make her forget that asshole.

He hated to admit it, but he'd been curious about her ex himself. He'd searched the dude online, scoped his social media. He had textbook douchebag written all over him. Financial manager at Sowell Banking by day, and member of the I-fuck-around-on-my-girlfriend-and-call-it-working-late club at night. Even without his current non-relationship with Carmen, he'd want to kick this guy's ass. Cocky, overconfident, swore he was God's gift to women.

"Is something wrong?"

He blinked a few times refocusing on Carmen. "Huh?"

She smiled nervously. "Where'd you go just now? You were cutting your steak and then just kept going like you wanted to saw the plate in half," she said.

Braxton looked down, and sure enough, there were silver scratch marks on the plate where his steak ended but he hadn't stopped cutting, Embarrassed, he set down the fork and knife and pushed his plate away.

"Are you done eating because I really want to fuck you a few good times before you get camera happy at the hotel," he said.

Fuck! That came out wrong.

He opened his mouth to apologize but Carmen's eyes glinted with lust and anticipation. She leaned forward and whispered into his ear.

"I think tonight maybe I can use my camera for more than just shots of the scenery."

"I like the sound of that," Braxton said. He dug out his wallet and tossed enough bills on the table to cover their meal before sliding out of the booth.

"I wasn't done eating," Carmen protested as he pulled her out of the booth as well.

"We'll get room service later," he said.

Carmen shook her head but didn't make a peep as he rushed them both out of the restaurant and to the hotel.

"You're trying to get us banned from another fancy hotel," Carmen laughed as Braxton tossed her onto the rose petal-covered bed.

She rolled over onto her hands and knees giving him the perfect view of her luscious ass. Carmen was already naked and glistening, primed from his fingers in the elevator and then his mouth against the door.

"My family supplied the lumber for these beds, handcrafted by me. Ain't shit breaking, no matter how rough I take you if that was my plan," Braxton said as he nudged her further up on the bed so he could position himself behind her.

She shuddered as he rubbed his cock along her slit, before rubbing her hand along the smooth reclaimed wood surface of the headboard. This bed he had hand-carved himself with the floral and heart motif the regency requested to match the décor of their honeymoon suite. Sturdy and beautiful. Watching her stroke and admire his work had the same effect as if she were doing it to the wood he was sporting just for her.

"Keep stroking that wood love, tell me how good it feels," he murmured in her ear as he thrust into her.

Carmen cried out gripping the headboard beneath her fingers, the ridges acted as convenient handholds for this exact purpose. He stroked in and out of her as she lovingly stroked his wooden creation. He'd had no idea how fucking hot he would be seeing this, being with her like this. Her head fell back against his shoulder and she arched her back. His hand found her clit, applying even pressure as his thrusts rubbed her against his hand.

"Braxton!" she screamed, her juices coating his dick and fingers.

She turned her head and he kissed her as he pounded out his own release and then he shifted them down the bed and under the covers.

"Sleep. I'll wake you in a bit so you can take your pictures," he said.

She nodded and closed her eyes, drifting to sleep. He watched her, not for the first time, but man did it feel different. His heart literally ached with how perfect she felt snuggled against him, her tiny fingers gripping his chest hair not as tightly as she did when he was buried in her, but with a definite possessiveness that he only just dared to encourage.

CHAPTER 7

Juice nearly shot out of Carmen's nose as Braxton did a cross between Magic Mike and the Chicken Dance. She thought he'd been lying about the fact he could not dance. The man, whose moves in the bedroom could not be ignored, now showed absolutely no rhythm. He couldn't even properly move his hips, let alone catch a beat.

He stopped gyrating like a washing machine on fast spin, a look of concern on his face.

"You alright over there, chuckles?"

Carmen wiped her face and took a deep breath. "Um, yeah. Just wow that was enlightening," she said forcing down another fit of laughter.

He sauntered over and knelt in front of her, his hazel eyes finding hers before a devious grin spread across his face. Carmen didn't even need to ask what was going through his head. Instead, she indulged him, leaning forward to kiss him. He slid closer, his massive frame pushing her legs apart in the process. The hot length of his erection pressed into her stomach.

"I can't believe a man with your talent in the bedroom would ever dance like that," she breathed.

"I'm really not that bad. I just figured I'd lighten the mood a bit after..." Braxton didn't need to finish the sentence.

His little dance routine had been prompted by a breach of their sex bubble by Carmen. They'd been talking about how pretty the fall morning was, and Carmen had reminisced about one of her happy memories with her parents before they'd slowly pushed her out of their lives. Before the small church her father started had grown to the massive money maker it was today. They'd gone out for a picnic in the park and her parents told her she was going to be an older sister.

They had all been so happy, laughing and joking. If only Carmen would have known her younger brother's birth would change all that for her. It seemed as soon as her father had learned he would have a son to pass on the family name, Carmen became a problem child. The memory was fine, the fact it had prompted her to explain to Braxton about why she wasn't close with her family was another. The conversation was too heavy for what they were doing and yet, he'd sat with her and had it anyway, before kissing her softly and asking if she'd ever seen an Edgewood Strip Tease.

Hilarity had ensued.

"You know I've been here two years and have never been to the amusement park on the river."

Braxton looked at her with shock. "Now that is something we need to remedy," he said standing.

He pulled Carmen from the chair and dragged her to the bedroom. Carmen fully expected another Braxton seduction as they showered and got dressed, but he was keeping his hands mostly to himself. Carmen was afraid she'd really killed the spark between them, but as soon as they were dressed, he pulled her into his arms and kissed her like his life depended on it.

"That should hold me over while we're in public," he said with a wink before leading her out of their hotel room.

Ping. Ping. Ping. Braxton easily took out three of the five metal targets at the shooting game.

"Still got it," he said, mostly to himself.

It had been a while since he'd shot anything. The Cross men's annual hunting trip had become more of a leisurely stroll through the trails with whiskey, beer and shit talk, than an actual hunting trip. He raised the literal pea shooter and took out the last two targets. The loud ringing signaling his win didn't bolster his ego the way that Carmen's proud smile did.

"I should have known you'd be good at this game," she laughed.

"You have your pick of the top prizes," the teenager manning the game said.

Braxton smiled down at Carmen. "You want one of those giant teddy bears?"

Carmen shook her head. "Even if I had any interest in a giant stuffed animal, there's no room for one where I'm staying now."

"What? You don't like stuffed animals?" Braxton could admit she was probably the first woman he'd ever gone out with who hadn't fawned over and begged for one of those giant fluffy things.

"They're cute and all, but with my allergies, all I see is a miserable allergen catcher waiting to ruin my day with puffy eyes and a runny nose," she said.

"Noted," he said and turned back to look at the shelf or prizes.

Braxton eyed the top shelf, there wasn't anything there he'd want to take home, and Carmen had already expressed her distaste for stuffed animals. He was about to settle on the purple and green basketball when he heard a little girl sniffling. He turned around spotting a young girl with two afro puffs standing in the middle of the walkway. Carmen had spotted her too and was already making her way over to the little girl.

"I think I'll take that giraffe right there," Braxton told the teen behind the counter.

"You sure? That's only a medium prize," the teen said.

"Yeah, just the giraffe."

The kid handed the stuffed animal over and Braxton caught up with Carmen and the little girl.

"She got separated from her older brother and his friends," Carmen said when he joined them. The little girl was still sniffling but was visibly calmer standing next to Carmen. Her eyes darted between him and the stuffed animal that matched the one on her t-shirt.

Braxton smiled down at the little girl.

"You want to hold onto this for me while we find your brother?" Braxton held out the giraffe and at first the little girl looked like she was going to refuse, but the moment passed. She grabbed the stuffed animal from his hand and held it tightly to her chest.

"What's the giraffe's name?" she asked.

Braxton shrugged. "To be honest we just met. Maybe you can get the giraffe to tell you their name while we walk to the information desk?"

"I think I can do that," the little girl said.

With that settled, Braxton took Carmen's hand in his and they walked through the park to the information desk by the entrance. Once the little girl was safely handed off to park staff, Carmen turned to Braxton.

"You're good with kids," she said.

"I'm really not. I just did all that to impress you," he said.

Carmen shook her head. "Sure, just keep trying to deny that you are big ole softy. I'm not buying it."

Braxton sighed and rubbed the back of his neck. "Kids are just tiny people. I treat them the same as anybody else."

He was blushing! Carmen had made Braxton, the dirty-talking mountain of a man, blush. Seeing him interact with the little girl had only further endeared her to him. She got close to him and fisted his shirt in her hands before pulling him down to her level.

"Does that blush of yours happen all over?"

Braxton looked confused for a second before his eyes darkened with understanding. He kissed the tip of her nose and gently loosened her grip on him.

"That's something you'll have to find out later. I promised myself I wouldn't have you caught up in bed all weekend, and I plan to keep that promise," he said.

Carmen blinked a few times before taking a step back. "Oh, I thought that was our arrangement. I mean, I like hanging out with you but sex was definitely the focus," she said.

"Our agreement was friends with benefits. Last weekend we focused on the benefits almost exclusively. I'd like to work on the friend part a bit more, if you don't mind," Braxton said.

If Carmen was reading Braxton's body language correctly, he was absolutely serious. With a shake of her head, Carmen grabbed Braxton's hand and pulled him back toward the center of the park. "Well, friend, I guess we should hit a ride or two."

Braxton was going to be sick. He should have known better than to ride the teacups twice in a row. He had barely been able to keep it together the first time around. Yet, he hadn't been able to deny Carmen's request. To be there as she whooped and giggled in delight while they spun around in circles.

"You're looking a little green. Are you okay?" Carmen grabbed his cheeks and smushed them together.

"No more teacups," he managed to mumble out.

She smiled at him and nodded toward the concession stand. "Why don't we grab you some water and take a break from the rides?"

"Yeah, that sounds like a plan," he said forcing himself upright. The world was still spinning a little but the concession stand was only a few steps away. He could make it there first, and then to a table to sit down for a second.

He took the first step and nearly fell over. His equilibrium was definitely shot. Carmen's teasing grin fell and her arms wrapped around his waist. "Why don't we just get you to a chair first? I'll get your water," she said.

Part of Braxton wanted to protest, put on some big man act, but the way his head was spinning he was man enough to admit when he needed a little help. So, he took short choppy steps as Carmen guided him to the nearest bench. She made sure he was okay before going to get in line. As soon as she was gone, Braxton closed his eyes and took several deep breaths.

"Boy, you are whipped! You know damn well you can't ride those things!" Braxton cringed at the sound of Hunter's voice.

He opened his eyes to see his cousin standing in front of him, holding hands with a young woman who barely looked old enough to be out of college. Not exactly who Braxton had pictured as the reason his cousin spent most of his time on this side of the mountain. No wonder Hunter was keeping this one a big secret. As accepting as their family was of his sexuality, this would surely send them into a marriage frenzy.

"Hello, Hunter's girlfriend. Nice to meet you. You should come visit the estate sometime," Braxton said without a smile.

If he smiled, he would throw up for sure, and that would be an even worse first impression than him being an unsmiling asshole.

"Vega's too busy," Hunter replied, not even giving the girl a chance to speak.

Braxton noticed Ms. Vega didn't even seemed bothered by Hunter's rudeness. Instead, she just kept smiling by his side even as her eyes traveled over Braxton. She was sizing him up, not in a sexual way but in the shrewd way women did with men who dated their friends. His suspicions were confirmed when she finally did speak.

"So, you're the one helping Carmen get over her ex." It was a statement not a question. Apparently, Braxton hadn't passed whatever metrics she had for friend's boyfriends.

"That I am," Braxton replied giving her his own once over, "and you're the one fake-dating my cousin."

She tensed at his accusation. Braxton was just making an assumption. Hunter operated under basically the same rule book Braxton had, until Braxton had met Carmen. Yet, the chemistry just wasn't there with the couple. They held hands but kept a good distance between themselves. The lack of interest on Vega's part about meeting anyone of Hunter's relatives. Yeah, they were definitely not intimate with each other at the very least. That was when Hunter shot Vega an apologetic look and confirmed Braxton's suspicions. Which brought up the bigger question. What was the draw for Hunter?

Braxton was just about to get all in their business when Carmen came over with the water for him. Vega pulled Hunter closer, her smile sliding into place as she snuggled with his cousin.

"Oh Carmen! I hope we didn't intrude on your date," the woman giggled.

Carmen smiled at the woman and shook her head. "It's not a date. We're just friends, but is this your mysterious boyfriend?"

Vega blushed and nodded. "I know I should bring him around more, but you know how my brother is. It makes dating hard."

Carmen just nodded. There was a ton of story here that Braxton didn't have and while normally he wasn't the gossiping type, he wanted to know more.

"Oh but you're out in the open now; that is so great for you two! Are you going to be at the Halloween party?" Carmen said.

Hunter didn't speak at first but then he blinked and turned to Vega. "Halloween Party?"

The was a fleeting flash of fear in Vega's eyes and then it was gone. "Oh, I hadn't had a chance to mention it. Yeah, we host a get-together the weekend before Halloween. Just a small gathering amongst friends and significant others. Nothing big," Vega said.

"Oh," Hunter said.

It was clear that he wasn't going to push an invite she didn't want to give. However, Carmen didn't seem to pick up on the obvious tension the subject had brought up.

"Vega, you are a grown woman with her own business. You shouldn't have to hide your relationship. Bring Hunter to the party, show your brother once and for all he can't bully you about this," Carmen said.

Vega sighed heavily, "You're right. Hunter, will you please be my date to the Halloween party?"

Hunter smiled at Vega but it didn't quite reach his eyes. "Of course, and in the spirit of not hiding relationships. I think Brax should come as Carmen's date."

Carmen opened her mouth as if she were going to refuse, but Braxton stood and wrapped his arm around Carmen's waist.

"Oh, I'm definitely there. I love parties and if things go south with Vega's brother, I can drag Hunter out of there," he offered.

Vega smiled at Braxton. "Then it's settled. I guess we'll see each other again, the weekend after next."

More small talk was exchanged before Hunter and Vega moved on to continue their so-called date. Braxton was suddenly very worried about the mess his little cousin had obviously gotten himself into. The whole situation was giving him the same icky feeling as when Baron told him Christine was pregnant. He'd almost lost his older brother to the crafty schemes of women. There was no way he'd sit idly watching his younger cousin fall the same way, especially since Hunter's father had made Braxton promise to look after Hunter before he died.

The memory of the accident only made Braxton feel worse. He leaned forward as bile rose in his throat. Closing his eyes, he took several slow deep breaths.

"Hey! You sure you're okay?" Carmen knelt beside him now, concern heavy in her voice.

She placed a hand on his shoulder. The small act of comfort was like a miracle salve. The sadness threatening to overcome him cleared away. Not entirely, but faster than it would have if he'd been left to pull himself together alone. He slowly lifted himself up, opening his eyes to meet her gaze.

"I'm good," he lied.

He wasn't good. He was better, but certainly not good. The brilliant smile he managed to throw at Carmen seemed to do the trick at selling it though, because she smiled back and continued chatting away.

"Hunter is your cousin, right?" Carmen asked.

"Yeah."

"Does he subscribe to the Wild Cross playbook too? Should I be worried for my friend?"

Braxton shook his head. "Normally, I'd say hell yeah, but in this case, I think my cousin is the one in need of worrying. Something's not right with what's going on there," Braxton said.

As soon as the words were out of his mouth, he regretted saying them. Carmen didn't seem like the type to take kindly to people talking bad about her friends. Case in point, she now stood in front of him, hands on her hips and a fire in her eyes that had nothing to do with wanting to kiss him.

"What's that supposed to mean?"

Braxton took a sip of the water she brought him and pointed to the Ferris Wheel. "Next ride, let's go."

He walked off before she could answer. Hell, he didn't even think she would follow him but she slid her hand into his as soon as he stepped into the line.

"You not pissed at me, or just holding it in because we're in public?"

"I was pissed but you're right. I don't know Vega very well but her personality is too passionate for there not to be obvious chemistry with anyone she'd dare go against her beloved brother to date in public."

Braxton nodded. "I think we should help them. I don't know how, but I don't want my cousin getting hurt and he wouldn't do something like this without good reason."

"Neither would Vega."

"So we're agreed? Our first couples project?"

Carmen rolled her eyes. "Friends helping friends project."

"Sure thing, babe."

"Don't call me, babe."

"Sugar tits?"

She glared at him and Braxton laughed.

"Babe it is then," he said.

"Noah called me babe."

That deflated Braxton real quick. "I'll just call you by your name, until we find something agreeable."

"Do you give all your friends pet names?"

"Nope, just the ones I fuck," Braxton replied.

"And how many is that?"

Braxton looked down at her a smug grin on his face. "So far, just you."

CHAPTER 8

She would not watch him go. *You will not watch him go.*

At the last second, she betrayed herself and turned around. Braxton hadn't left yet. He was standing by his truck, watching her go up the stairs to Imena's apartment. She'd refused to let him walk her to the door. That was much too date-like and yet, here they were. Like two lovesick teens, anxious at the idea of being apart for any amount of time. He smiled at her and waved. She awkwardly waved back before jogging up the last few stairs and letting herself in with the key Imena gave her.

The apartment wasn't empty as she expected. Not only was Imena home but Scarlett was there as well.

"Amayah's on her way," Imena said.

Carmen crossed her arms over her chest. "To what do I owe this ambush? Clearly, this isn't a hang otherwise you would have given me a heads up."

"Before I get into that, the apartment manager came by. There is a studio in this complex that will be available by the end of next week. She knew you were looking and wanted to offer it to you before she put out an ad," Imena said.

"Of course, I'm interested! Sorry, it's not that I don't love you and your hospitality, but I can't wait to sleep in my own bed for once. I went from my parents to a dorm and then I moved in with Noah. I'll finally be able to decorate to my taste," Carmen said.

"Yes! We should definitely go shopping as soon as you get the lease signed," Scarlett said.

"Okay, but now to the reason we are all gathered. Vega texted me about your date at the amusement park yesterday," Imena said.

Carmen's jovial mood at the possibility of getting her own space quickly evaporated. "It wasn't a date. We went as friends."

"Friends who hold hands and cuddle in line?" Scarlett said.

Carmen marched over to the kitchen and pulled out Imena's stash of tequila. "I need a drink for this," she grumbled.

"Hey! We're just a little worried? I mean, I know we were the ones who pushed you to have this fling. We cosigned it even. We just don't want you to rush into another relationship is all," Amayah said, coming through the front door.

"It's not a relationship. We agreed to be friends with benefits. Besides, if you guys are so worried you can see for yourselves at the Halloween party."

"You're bringing him to the Halloween party? This I have to see," Scarlett laughed.

"It's not a big deal. Anyway, Vega probably brought all this up to pull attention away from the fact she's in some kind of situation with Hunter Cross," Carmen said.

Imena rolled her eyes. "That will resolve itself soon. Don't deflect."

"No, please do deflect, what's going on with that? Hunter is not the relationship type." Scarlet leaned forward, interest shining in her eyes.

"Braxton thinks they are fake dating, but neither of us can figure out why they would go along with that," Carmen said, ignoring Imena.

Scarlett sat back the sparkle clearly gone from her eyes. "Oh that, well, my best guess is Hunter wants revenge on Florian Falconer for rejecting him so harshly, but I can't see why Vega would be willing to go against her brother like that."

"Rejecting him, romantically?" Carmen asked.

"Oh yeah, they used to share women occasionally, but rumor has it Hunter wanted to stop sharing and just keep Florian. Florian tried to let Hunter down gently, but you are aware of how persistent Cross men can be when they want something," Scarlett said.

"Vega would never date Hunter knowing he was involved with Florian. Fake or not," Imena said.

"She's dating Hunter to make Jacinto jealous. I mean, it's obvious she's in love with him to anyone who is around them for longer than half a second." Amayah said.

"Ugh, we shouldn't gossip like this. Vega is our friend. Imena's best friend. We should help her with this instead," Carmen said.

"I'll admit I knew about the fake dating and didn't push, but now that I know about the Hunter Florian connection there is no way I can't interfere. I'm texting Vega right now," Imena said.

While Imena texted back and forth with Vega, Amayah and Scarlett joined Carmen in taking shots of liquor.

"I'm kind of jealous of your agreement with Braxton," Scarlett said after the third shot.

"Why? You could have any man you set your eyes on," Amayah said.

"Not any man. Am I the only one who knows about your crush on Chef Kim?" Carmen said.

"Are you still stalking him?" Amayah asked.

"It's not stalking! I honestly do enjoy his food that much to eat at either Flower Café or Sowell Garden at least twice a week. Anyway, we are talking about Carmen right now not me," Scarlett said.

Carmen shrugged. "There is nothing really to talk about."

"Really? I mean, he chased Noah out of a restaurant for you." Imena joined in.

"He did what now?" Amayah gasped.

"Oh yeah, apparently on their first date, Noah showed up and Braxton got all in his face and nearly made him pee his pants," Imena said.

"Man, I wish I had been there to see that!" Amayah said.

"That is not what happened," Carmen said.

"Sounds exactly like something Braxton would do. You wanna continue lying about your not relationship?" Scarlett scoffed.

Carmen didn't answer. She just rolled her eyes and poured them all another shot. It was clear that no amount of explanation would convince her friends that she and Braxton weren't a couple. They'd made up their minds and if Carmen was being honest with herself, despite everything, Carmen wished she were in the right headspace to actually date Braxton. Like he'd said at the restaurant, things happened the way they did for a reason. She only wished the timing of his arrival into her life wasn't so shitty.

Braxton swore when he saw Baron sitting on his front porch barefoot and in his boxers. It was still early in fall and while the days were warm, the nights were getting frigid. He parked his truck and climbed out. It was then he noticed the empty bottle of whiskey at his brother's feet.

"You alright, Baron?"

Baron looked up at him, a slow grin spreading across his face. "No! I need another bottle. I'm celebrating!"

"Celebrating what? Christine sign the divorce papers?"

Baron's smile turned into a pained grimace. "Fuck no. She's still holding out for more money. Money I don't fucking have cuz the vampire bitch has drained me dry."

"So what are we celebrating?" Braxton said sitting down on the porch next to his brother.

There was no way he was going inside and risking his stash of thirty-year-old scotch, or his brother getting alcohol poisoning.

"I'm celebrating the end of my delusions about Christine. As well as contemplating filing for bankruptcy."

Braxton skipped right over the landmine of anything involving Christine and focused on the latter part of his brother's slurred sentence. He'd known Christine had run up a few credit cards and took a loan or two out in Baron's name, but he hadn't realized it was bad enough for Baron to file for bankruptcy. Baron got paid good money. He'd driven the same old truck since high school and built the home he lived in himself. Well, with help from Braxton, Bechet, and Hunter. Those had been fun times, back when they'd all been thick as thieves. Before the pressures of adulthood and familial obligation mucked things up.

"Bankruptcy, huh. Why would you want to celebrate being a broke dick," Braxton said.

Baron laughed. "*Broke dick*! I am a broke dick. I ain't got no money and I haven't had a decent erection in three damn years."

On that note, Braxton grabbed his brother by the arm and hauled him up. No way, Baron would ever say such a thing unless he was drunk out of his mind. Not that Braxton had any doubt about that considering, he was naked and three sheets to the wind sitting on his front porch. They were close but hadn't been that close for a few years now; Baron had done a good job of erecting walls around himself in the last year that no one but Hunter had managed to get through.

The love was still there, of course. They were brothers and he understood that Baron had gone through some serious shit, more than even Braxton had realized considering the news his brother was 'celebrating'. So, like a good little brother he would make sure this little episode was one that stayed between the both of them. Sure, he could carry Baron to his own place and tuck him in. Let him wake up with no memory of the night and feeling sorry for himself but after the last bout of depression that had forced the family to step in and get Baron some serious mental health support, Braxton wasn't taking any chances. He hefted his older brother's weight up the remaining stairs and into Braxton's cabin.

"I can walk my damn self," Baron said pulling out of Braxton's grasp.

"Sure, you can. I just want to make sure you don't walk your damn self into a wall." Braxton dropped his brother on the couch and went to the kitchen to grab him and aspirin and a glass of water.

"Thank you," Baron said downing both, before he passed out.

Braxton got a woven throw from his linen closet and tossed it over his brother before grabbing his scotch and taking it into his bedroom for the night. He tucked the bottle safely in his underwear drawer, just in case Baron woke up during the night and went hunting for a nightcap. Seeing Baron so messed up over Christine was a reminder of why he'd stuck to his playbook all these years. He hadn't wanted to end up like his brother, never wanted to give any woman the power to wreck him so completely.

Then what are you doing with Carmen?

Braxton paused at the thought. He honestly had no idea. He just knew that right now if he walked away from her, he'd regret it. So yeah, he was willing to risk ending up like his brother, just to see how things ended up. Carmen hadn't thrown any red flags his way yet, and he wanted to trust that not all women were like Christine and those from his past.

He changed into his pajamas and settled into bed before texting Carmen.

B: Made it home. Sweet Dreams, Carmen.

CHAPTER 9

*D*ing. *Dong. Ding. Dong.* Carmen's alarm wasn't normally that loud. She didn't need much to wake her in the morning but today the chiming bells, felt like she was standing in the middle of a giant cathedral's bell tower. She reached over to silence the cacophony.

How much did I fucking drink?

The answer was way too much. Last night had gone from a Braxton intervention to an all-out drag fest of men. Aided by copious amounts of tequila and vodka. With a groan she pushed herself up from the couch, swinging her feet down only to come in contact with another human instead of the Berber carpet.

"Shit, sorry," she hissed moving her feet back up.

Her apology fell on deaf ears. Scarlett and Amayah were curled up on the floor next to the couch. At least, she wasn't going to be the only one hating life today. She carefully crawled over the arm of the couch to avoid stepping on her friends and made her way to the kitchen. She needed water and an aspirin and coffee. Especially the coffee. She was in desperate need of coffee.

She frowned at the time on Imena's coffee maker as she loaded the top with enough grounds to make a full pot. She wasn't the only one who would need a cup or two this morning. The numbers however didn't make any sense. Carmen's alarm didn't go off until 7am. The clock read 5am which was only about three hours after she'd passed out on the couch.

Ding. Dong. Ding. Dong. That was not her alarm. It had to be Amayah's. She was the only one whose job and commute required her to be awake at this hour.

With a groan, Amayah lifted her head from the floor. "Where am I?"

"Imena's apartment. You might want to call off for the day or at least take a half day," Carmen grumbled.

Amayah nodded and silenced her phone before going back to sleep. Carmen wished she could go back to sleep. She needed the rest but that wasn't how she worked. Once her body was up, she was up, hangover or not. With coffee on the way, she made her way to the bathroom to shower and change for the day. She didn't have any appointments at the studio until the afternoon and since she was up so early, she couldn't resist trying to get a few sunrise shots in.

The question was from where? It would take too long to make it to the Sowell Gate. She could go down by the river, maybe take a few morning shadow shots of the Buchanon-Hancock District. She smiled at the possibilities there with their cobblestone streets and eclectic architecture. Not to mention she could snag some pastries from Flower Café. Refreshed from her shower, and morning planned, Carmen slipped out before her friends woke up and held her up with more chat about Braxton or whatever.

She loved her friends, appreciated their concern, but nothing helped Carmen sort out her shit better than indulging in her work. She parked her Jeep outside of Shampooches, the dog grooming salon owned by Amayah's boyfriend Yarrow. She'd never been inside because of her allergies but knew it was a safe place to park so she wouldn't have to waste money on parking fees and wouldn't get towed if she was parked a little too long.

The sun had started to rise as she parked, the early rays a vibrant orange that darkened into a deep purple. She smiled to herself. This was exactly what she needed. She let herself get lost behind the camera, roaming the near-empty streets, snapping away to her heart's content until the sun had fully risen and the sweet smells from Flower Café made her empty stomach rumble.

Despite it being Monday morning and super early, there was already a line forming out front. Their food was that good. Carmen got in line and pulled out her phone. She wondered if it was too early to text Braxton. If she did, was that blurring the lines of friendship and relationship? She opened her messenger and saw his text from the night before wishing her sweet dreams and smiled. Her fingers moved before her brain could stop her.

C: Alcohol killed any dreams I would have had last night, sweet or otherwise.

She hit send and then cringed wishing she hadn't. Why couldn't she have written something cute and witty instead of basically admitting she'd gotten shit-faced and passed out.

B: The girls liquored you up for info huh?

C: How did you know?

B: Vega seemed like the type to blab about others' business. I'm surprised they waited until I dropped you off instead of calling during our time.

C: Our time?

B: Yes, weekends are our time. At least your friends respect that.

Carmen leaned against the brick wall.

C: Did you have sweet dreams?

B: Sweet? No. Wet? Most definitely. I dreamt about you all night and woke up to a mess in my bed. You should come visit me this weekend so I can make a mess of you instead.

C: I guess we have done two weekends on my side of the mountain. If I say yes does this mean I'll be meeting more of your family?

B: Not unless you really want to. I have my own cabin far enough from the main house that we could spend the whole weekend without running into a single other person if we didn't want to.

C: You sure you're not trying to trick me to your mountain shack, with plans of shackling me to your bed and keeping me as your sex slave?

Oh god, You are being so extra and weird right now? Why are you like this Carmen?

B: My place isn't a shack, it's a very nice cabin. Although shackling you to my bed is in the plans. I promise to let you go once Our Time is up.

C: There you go with that Our Time stuff. Fine, I'll make the trip, but you better show me some of those views you bragged about. I'm bringing my camera.

B: You like Our Time, admit it. Anyway, I'll send you directions and stuff later.

C: Sounds like a plan

B: It's a date

Carmen would have melted into the brick wall if it weren't for the fact the open sign flipped on the front door of Flower Café and she was forced to pull her head out of her Braxton fog and move.

"What's got you grinning like the cat who got the cream?"

Braxton looked up from his coffee to glare at his older brother. Baron was sitting up on the couch, his brown hair a disheveled mess.

"None of your business. If you want to shower here, you can borrow my sweats. If not, you have about ten minutes before your window for an unseen walk back to your place is gone," Braxton said.

Baron ran a hand over his face before standing up. He walked over to the kitchen and fixed himself a cup of coffee. "I don't remember much about last night. I just know it never happened."

"Sure, you came over this morning in your skivvies cuz all your clothes were torn to shreds by a bear," Braxton snorted.

"Weirder things have happened," Baron shrugged downing the black coffee like it wasn't piping hot, before walking out the front door.

Braxton shook his head. Baron was a real piece of work. He didn't want his brother to fall under another woman's spell anytime soon, but after last night Baron knew that a major step in his older brother getting over his trifling ex would be to get under someone new. He switched from his thread with Carmen to his private one with Hunter and Bechet.

B: We need to get Baron laid.

Chet: We need to do what now?

Bechet didn't go by Chet anymore but Braxton kept him listed in his phone that way just to piss him off.

H: It is too GD early for you to be sending me nonsense.

B: If it's too early why are you answering?

Chet: Hunter your ass needs to be up getting ready for work, slacker

H: I'm turning off my phone.

B: Baron's divorce is in the works and he may have admitted to me that he hasn't had sex in three years.

Chet: Not my problem. I'm out.

H: I'll take him to a bar or something this weekend. That's too fucking long, no wonder he's off his shit.

B: Also, he talked about filing for bankruptcy

H: Fuck

B: But you didn't hear it from me

Chet: Fucking Baron. Always acting like his shit don't stink and he's a fucking broke ass cuckold.

B: Watch your mouth young man. He's still your older brother.

Chet: I'm allowed my opinion

H: You sure? I thought you were only allowed Isis' opinion now

Chet: I thought you were turning off your phone

B: Hey! Baron needs our help. Can we focus?

Chet: He may need our help but he doesn't want it. At least not from me. You two are on your own with this one. Also, Brax we still need to talk about the Corinthian incident.

H: Is that what we're calling Carmen?

B: Fuck off

Chet: So the cosplay rumors were true?

H: Oh yeah and get this her real name is Carmen too!

B: Bechet I'll call you later. Hunter get your lazy ass out of bed and come help me in the workshop.

Braxton exited out of the thread and finished his breakfast in a rush. He wanted to get to his workshop and get some work done before he handled Hunter.

Carmen was too busy daydreaming about seeing Braxton again that weekend. If she hadn't been, she would have seen both Scarlett approach her and the glares of the people behind her as Scarlett slid into the line.

"Hey doll, thanks for saving me a spot," Scarlett said cheerily.

Carmen blinked a few times before shaking her head at her friend. "Ugh, how can you be so chipper when you drank double what I did?"

"My line of work thrives on bar culture and drinking. I kinda have to have a high tolerance. Anyway, Chef Kim is here today; I can't help but be happy when I get to see him in the morning."

"Should I be concerned about you? I mean, stalking is a crime." Carmen was only half-joking.

"It's not stalking it's admiration from a distance. He's just so cute and his food is amazing. He's great with people." Scarlett was getting starry-eyed as she spoke.

"But he has already said he wasn't interested," Carmen pointed out.

"He didn't say he wasn't interested exactly, he just said he didn't have time to date," Scarlett said.

Carmen rolled her eyes and was about to point out that the Chef had probably been trying to let her down gently, when the man himself walked right up to them. He had a genuine smile as he handed Scarlett a to go cup and bag of pastries.

"Your usual order. I wanted to make sure you got your faves before they ran out. You're usually here earlier than this," Chef Kim said.

Scarlet smiled back, their hands lingering on each other's just a second longer than necessary to handle the exchange of goods.

"Girls' night got a bit out of hand. Thank you, I know you're busy; you really didn't have to do this," Scarlett said.

"I am busy, but I was already headed out to the main restaurant. It was nothing to grab these for you on the way out. You're one of our most loyal customers. I mean, it was my pleasure." Chef Kim blushed and ran his hand nervously over the back of his neck.

Carmen looked between her friend and her crush. Maybe Carmen was wrong to have judged Scarlett's insistence on hanging around. Maybe Chef Kim *was* interested and truly just didn't have the time. Especially considering he was helping manage two very successful restaurants in town.

The two of them stared longingly at each other before Chef Kim cleared his throat. "I have to get going."

"Right, I don't want to keep you," Scarlett managed to pull herself together.

Chef Kim nodded and took off leaving Carmen and Scarlett alone. Well, not really alone as they were standing in line still. The people around them gawked enviously as Scarlett sipped the coffee her crush had brought directly to her. Thankfully, the line started to move faster and soon Carmen had her own coffee and pastries to enjoy.

They managed to get a seat inside since most people were taking their food to go and sat down. Carmen had a few minutes to spare before she would need to get to her studio to set up. Scarlett decided she could miss the last thirty minutes of her class since she was already too late to dare show up to the lecture hall.

"Okay, I take back what I said about him not being interested," Carmen said.

Scarlet smirked at her. "Good, now we can focus on what costume you and Brax are going to wear to the Halloween party. It has to be something totally epic."

Carmen scowled. "I think that whatever he chooses to wear will be fine."

"Oh, come on Carmen, why are you passing up this golden opportunity to do a cute couples costume. I remember last year how you complained that Noah refused to dress up saying it was for kids."

"Because a couple's costume is for couples. Braxton and I are just friends."

"Ugh, lies. Anyway, it doesn't matter. Friends dress up together too. Remember last year we went as the twins from The Shining?"

"That was fun. Although last year's party theme was horror movies. This one is superheroes and I don't think Braxton is the type of guy who'd wear tights."

"He's not, but I would love to see it."

"Of course you would," Carmen laughed.

To be honest, Carmen hadn't even thought about costumes for the party yet. Not even her own. She wondered if Braxton was like Noah and would refuse to wear a costume, or if he would want to do a group costume with her. She refused to call it a couple's costume given their situation. She mentally filed it away as something to discuss with him that weekend when she visited Edgewood. Actually, she should probably give him a bigger heads-up than just a week to pull together a costume. A man his size would need time to find something good.

Carmen pulled out her phone and texted him.

C: I almost forgot to tell you the Halloween party is a costume party and the theme is superheroes

"Are you asking him?" Scarlett leaned over the table to peer at Carmen's phone. Carmen set her phone down not expecting Braxton to answer if he was busy with work.

"Yes, nosy." Her phone buzzed and Scarlett flipped it over.

"Aww, he replied almost immediately. You can't tell me that's not boyfriend behavior," Scarlett gushed.

"He's attentive, sure, but again *not* my boyfriend." Carmen unlocked her phone not bothering to shield the message from Scarlett, who made no effort to hide that she was reading the screen.

B: I love a good costume party. I'll put together a few ideas and we can compare notes this weekend.

"See I told you he'd be down for a couple's – I mean friends' – costume."

C: Compare notes?

B: So we don't clash. I mean going as a team would be preferred but if not I'd at last like to go within the same fandom. Like If I'm Captain America and you go as Wonder Woman that would be tragic.

"That would be tragic. I mean if he goes Marvel and you go DC."

"I don't even know what you're talking about," Carmen said.

Scarlett gasped, "How are we even friends if you don't know the difference between Marvel and DC?"

"Because we are both greater than our knowledge of pop culture," Carmen said.

C: I'm not that into Wonder Woman so I think you'd be safe there

B: So sad you would be smokin' hot as wonder woman and I'd totally let you lasso the fuck out of me later

"You totally have to go as Wonder Woman now. How could you pass up that blatant innuendo," Scarlett said.

Carmen snorted with laughter. "Easily. I don't need a lasso of truth to tie that man up. Although it may have come in handy with Noah. I could have avoided so much with a tool like that."

C: Do I need to tie you up for you to tell me the truth? You got something to hide?

B: I've got nothing to hide but you can tie me up all you want when you come visit me this weekend.

"He invited you to the estate!" Scarlett squealed but Carmen ignored her.

C: Good to know. I'll bring my notes and my cuffs.

She tucked her phone away, not wanting Scarlett to see whatever else Braxton would reply with.

"Uh, yeah, why?"

"Dude, the boys don't bring women to the compound unless it's serious."

"It isn't serious. He's just going to show me a few hiking trails," Carmen said.

"Private trails that can only be accessed from their property. The only woman I know who's ever gotten access like that was Christine, and she had to get pregnant to do it," Scarlett said.

"Christine?" Carmen hated the sudden clench of her stomach at the thought of someone else with Braxton.

"Oh, you don't have to worry about her. She got her hooks into Baron Cross, Braxton's oldest brother. Anyway, all I'm saying is that for someone who swears she isn't getting caught up with Braxton, there seems to be a whole lot of couple activity going on," Scarlett said.

Carmen sighed.

"If you're right, should I cancel? Should I make up an excuse not to hang out with him this weekend?"

"Hell, no! Go and enjoy the views and the hot sex and anything else you two do together. I just want you to know that despite what you two might have agreed upon, Braxton isn't treating you like he treated the others. I'm glad, but I also can't help but worry. I feel like the chances of one or both of you getting hurt at the end of this is too high," Scarlett said.

"Noted."

The anime theme song that was Scarlett's ring tone began to chime. She pulled her bedazzled pink phone case from her purse and scowled.

"Shit, I gotta run. We'll catch up later this week maybe? If not have fun in Edgewood. I mean it!"

She was already out of her chair and out the door before Carmen could respond. Looking at her own phone, Carmen needed to get a move on herself, she wanted to talk with the apartment manager before going to her studio.

"You're distracted," Bechet said with a frown.

Braxton put a hand over his face and nodded. This was exactly why he hated video calls. There was no hiding when Bechet got caught up in all the details of contracts and numbers and Braxton inevitably checked out. Usually, he would be envisioning his next masterpiece. Today, however, his mind kept drifting back to the image of Carmen in a Wonder Woman costume sprawled out on a bed beneath him.

"So, Hunter was right about this woman. Carmen, right?"

"I don't know what you're talking about," Braxton huffed.

Bechet had the nerve to laugh. "Listen, wasn't it you who was just riding my ass for being distracted by Isis? Do yourself a favor and make things official with her. The longer you keep pretending you don't want her like that, the worse it's going to get. Trust me."

"I know you are high on newlywed vibes so I'm just going to ignore what you just said. Anyway, I've wrapped up the last of the first order from the Corinthian and have sent Margo a few sketches for the economy line."

"Good, I'm glad I don't have to ream your ass for messing up this deal for us. Now tell me about this woman," Bechet said.

"Carmen is great. She's funny and sweet. Likes the outdoors. She's an amazing photographer," Braxton said.

"Wow, Hunter is right. You do have a girlfriend."

"What do you mean?"

"Usually when you talk about women you call them anything but their name, broad, chick, hottie etc... Then you proceed to brag about how you two fucked twelve ways to Sunday before you drop their ass."

Braxton frowned.

"I'm not really that bad, am I?"

"Oh yeah, where do you think Hunter got it from bro?"

"Fuck, well regardless. Things are different with Carmen. We are friends first, even if we started off mostly with the benefits."

"Even worse, need I remind you I tried to do the friends with benefits thing with Isis?"

"You're different though. You were always more the relationship type. I do like Carmen a lot, but right now the best I can do is just try not to fuck things up."

"Most men claim not to be the relationship type until they find the one they want to be in a relationship with. As far as not fucking things up, I'm not exactly the best person to help with that. All I can say is actions speak louder than words. So, if you really want something long-term with Carmen, make sure you act like it, even when you can't express it with words."

Hunter chose that moment to come striding into Braxton's workshop.

"Hunter just got here, let me call you back," Braxton hung up before Bechet could say anything more.

It wasn't that he was hiding his conversation from his cousin, but rather that Hunter didn't look like his usually jovial self. His mouth was set into a scowl and his brow was furrowed as if deep in thought. Hunter never thought too deeply about anything. At least not when others were around.

"I was gonna rip you a new one, but it looks like someone already beat me to it," Braxton said.

Hunter turned his scowl on Braxton, a glint of anger in his eyes.

"You and your girlfriend need to keep your noses out of other people's business," he snapped.

Braxton straightened at Hunter's tone and squared off with the younger man. "I don't know what bug crawled up your ass but say anything bad about Carmen and you'll regret it," he hissed.

Hunter rolled his eyes. "Don't need to puff up on me. All I'm saying is that things between Vega and me were fine until your girl pulled this mess about Halloween," Hunter grumbled.

"That's not on Carmen. You and Vega both could have said no."

"If I had said no then you two would have been suspicious," Hunter said.

Braxton laughed. "I could give two shits if you want to fake date some chick. If she weren't Carmen's friend, I wouldn't be involved at all," Braxton said.

"Well, it doesn't matter, we ain't dating anymore. Fake or otherwise thanks to you," Hunter said.

Braxton couldn't help the immediate relief he felt over that situation being done with. "What does it matter unless you actually liked the girl and the whole fake dating scheme was just a means to an end."

"Vega's great; there might have been something eventually but I didn't get that chance."

Braxton shook his head.

"So, let me get this straight. You are mad because your *not* girlfriend, who you didn't even like that way, decided to end things because she also didn't feel that way about you?"

Hunter looked up at the ceiling, his jaw working like he was chewing on a piece of gum. It was a habit he had since he was little and trying to figure out if he should lie or tell the truth. "Fuck you, man. What do you need help with?"

"I was going to ask your help with costume ideas for this party but since you're obviously not going..."

Hunter flicked Braxton off. "Go as Sasquatch you hairy bastard."

"Fine, I guess I'll have to get Baron to help."

CHAPTER 10

Carmen's trip to Edgewood didn't happen. The studio apartment had come available sooner than expected and almost as soon as she'd gotten the keys, Carmen managed to come down with a cold. Braxton had offered to come and stay with her, nurse her back to health but she'd begged off. Maybe this was a sign that things had gone beyond their original agreement and she needed to slow things down.

Still, as she lay miserable and alone in her nearly empty space, she wished he were there with her. Imena had offered to let her stay at her place until she was better, but Carmen hadn't wanted to risk getting any of her friends sick either. Not that her friends seemed to have received the memo to stay away. Amayah had come by with juice and medicine; Scarlett had dropped by with hot soup from Sowell Garden; Imena had brought over a special blend of herbal tea and a tea kettle since Carmen hadn't had a chance to do any of the shopping she'd planned on doing.

Carmen pulled her sleeping bag tighter around her as another wave of chills hit her. Maybe she should have taken Imena's offer to stay on her couch. Laying on the cold hard floor wasn't doing her aching body any favors. Carmen closed her eyes, maybe if she could take another nap. It felt like just two minutes later when there was a pounding on her door.

"Carmen! Carmen!" It was Braxton.

She groaned and tried to roll her weak, sweaty body off the floor, to no avail. She glanced at her phone which showed not only had her short nap turned into an all-day sleep, but that she'd missed calls and messages from nearly everyone. Her door suddenly swung open and Braxton came barreling inside, followed by Imena, Scarlett, and Amayah.

Carmen had given Imena a spare key in case of emergencies but Carmen hadn't thought she'd have need to use it, especially not this soon. Braxton scooped her up from the floor with little effort and pressed his hand against her forehead.

"I'm taking her to the hospital," he said.

"I don't need a hospital," Carmen muttered.

Braxton glared down at her, concern shining brighter than the anger she saw there. "I wasn't asking."

"Go, we'll lock up here and meet you there," Imena said.

Carmen turned her head to glare at her friend but the movement made her head spin and the next thing she knew she was emptying her already empty stomach all over Braxton and herself. He carried her to the kitchen sink.

"Still, want to protest?" Braxton said holding back her hair.

Carmen shook her head and Braxton pulled off his dirty shirt before picking her up again. She snuggled into his broad chest as he carried her to his truck. Scarlett followed with Carmen's purse, while Amayah and Imena stayed behind to clean up the mess.

"Take care of my girl, Brax," Scarlett said as Braxton shrugged on a clean shirt he conveniently had in his back seat.

"*My* girl and I will see you at the hospital," Braxton said.

Braxton sat in the waiting room with Amayah, Imena and Scarlett. Carmen was being seen by the doctors and, since he wasn't family nor her boyfriend, he'd been sent to wait outside while she was examined.

"You didn't have to drive all the way out here, but thank you," Amayah said to him.

"To be honest, I was already on my way. A few of the workers at the factory caught this cold and I knew it wouldn't be just a simple case of the sniffles. I also wanted to get measurements of her place, so I could make her housewarming gift," Braxton said.

Imena smiled at him. "I knew you were going to be good for our Carmen."

"He still has plenty of time to fuck things up," Scarlett said.

Braxton shot her a glare but she just smiled and cuffed his shoulder. "I'm kidding! Kind of. Honestly, I'm glad that you are serious about her; just don't make me regret it," she clarified.

"I definitely don't plan on hurting her. I care about her, but I also know she needs time to get over her ex. I appreciate your support though," he said.

"Noah isn't really the issue. I mean, he did a number on her for sure, but she isn't grieving that relationship in the least. She went from her strict parents' rule into a controlling relationship. I think she just needs time to come into her own," Scarlett said.

"Yeah, she told me a bit about her parents and I saw how things with Noah were when I helped her move out. That's why I'm trying to take things slow, why I didn't immediately come on Friday when she told me she wasn't feeling well."

"Fuck slow, you two are meant to be. Why fight it?" Imena said.

"Imena!" Amayah gasped.

"What? Normally I try not to pry or interfere based on things I've seen but, in this case, I just can't help it. I want the happy ending for Carmen," Imena said.

Braxton frowned and raised an eyebrow at the three women as they began to discuss Imena's supposed psychic abilities, and all the ways she'd been wrong or right about things in the past. Thankfully, at that moment Carmen came out of the exam room with a sheet of paper in her hand.

"I can't believe you all are still here," she said.

Braxton stood and pulled her into his arms. It was a relief to see her up and obviously feeling better. Carmen snuggled into him, and he silently thanked himself for already having a bag packed for the weekend, so he'd been able to change into a clean shirt.

"What did the doctors say?" Amayah said.

Carmen pulled away just enough to face her friends, but he noticed, with more than a little delight, that she didn't pull away from his embrace.

"It's a simple cold. I just got dehydrated which made things worse. A little IV drip and I'm good to go," she said.

"Thank god! Next time you get sick, we are not leaving you to your own devices," Scarlett said.

"Next time she gets sick, I'll be right there to take of her. Don't you worry," Braxton said.

The comment earned smiles from Carmen's friends, but a pinch in the side from Carmen.

"I can handle myself. This just happened to be a set of unfortunate circumstances," she huffed.

"Avoidable circumstances," he shot back.

She tried to pull away from him but he kept her firmly by his side.

"Well, Braxton. We see that you have things handled here, so we'll leave you two lovebirds to it," Imena said and grabbed both Scarlett and Amayah's arms, dragging them out of the hospital.

Braxton pulled Carmen along as well, since she was discharged. She didn't speak to him as they got into his truck, or even as they pulled out of the hospital parking lot and headed in the opposite direction to her new apartment.

"You're not going to ask where I'm taking you?" he asked.

Carmen waved her hand in the air. "I figured you'd probably gotten a hotel room with plans of seducing me or something," she said.

Braxton sighed. "The thought crossed my mind, but no. We aren't going to a hotel. We are going to the store to get you a temporary bed, so you aren't sleeping on the damn floor," he said.

Carmen grimaced. "I can't go shopping in this." She gestured toward her rumpled sweaty pajamas.

"No worries. I've already bought everything. We're just going to pick it up."

"That was very presumptuous of you," she scowled.

"I think the phrase you're looking for is 'thank you'. I mean, I know you want to pack out your own things. It's your home but I can't in good conscience let you sleep on the floor in a sleeping bag when you are ill. It's taking everything in me, not to just take you back to my place and keep you there until I'm satisfied that you're healthy enough to take care of things yourself," he said.

Carmen remained pouty and grouchy with him until he'd finished putting together her new bed in her tiny studio apartment. It was just a simple metal frame and mattress set, but as soon as he'd gotten the new blankets all laid out he turned to see Carmen standing next to him in tears.

"Thank you, Braxton," she said quietly.

He gave her a quick hug before urging her to get under the covers. "Thank me by getting some rest so you can get better."

With her tucked in, he moved over to the small kitchen area and poured some freshly boiled water over the packet of herbs that Imena had left for Carmen. Looking at the leaves, he was reminded of the tea his Aunt Mirna always brought over when he or his brothers got sick as kids. Now the whole conversation about Imena's psychic abilities made sense. The woman was a witch; not that Braxton actually believed in all that, but he knew that this tea would make Carmen better from his own experience.

He brought her the cup and watched her take a few sips before she settled into her new bed.

"Are you not going to join me?" she asked.

"I want to, but I know that if I get in bed with you now, I won't be able to leave."

"Who said I wanted you to leave," she purred.

"I didn't think you wanted me to stay. You've been pretty cross with me since I showed up uninvited. I mean, I understand if you need some space," he said.

"So, one second you're barging in and demanding to take care of me and now you're saying you understand if I need some space? Braxton, that doesn't make any sense."

"I know it doesn't. I want to stay. I want to take care of you. I just don't want to further overstep. If you want me to go I will."

"I don't want you to go. I told you to stay away, not because I needed space but because I didn't want to get you sick. You came anyway, have been fully exposed since I puked on you, so you might as well stay. I want you to stay," she said.

Braxton smiled and grabbed his keys off the counter.

"So you're leaving?" Carmen sounded hurt.

He walked over to the bed and pressed a kiss on her forehead. "I'm not leaving. I'm just going to get my overnight bag from the truck," he said.

A few minutes later, Braxton was in his pajamas and crowding Carmen in the full-size bed he'd bought for her. His massive frame barely fit and she was forced to be practically on top of him, not that she minded. Between whatever magic Imena had put in that tea and the warmth of Braxton's body beneath her, Carmen felt much better.

"I know you were busy this week, but did you get a chance to come up with some costume ideas?" Braxton was trying to keep their conversation light. A distraction from the heavy sexual tension between them.

Carmen laughed. "Ugh, yes. Scarlett sent me an entire essay about the difference between DC and Marvel characters and what constitutes a superhero," Carmen said.

Braxton tensed underneath her.

"You really didn't know the difference before? I thought you were joking?"

"Religious parents remember. The only superhero I was allowed to be familiar with was Our Lord and Savior," she said.

"Right but when you left, you never watched the films or anything?"

Carmen shrugged. "Noah always said theaters were too expensive and that respectable women didn't indulge in violent films," Carmen said.

"What an asshole! Anyway, I at least know what we are doing today. Where is your laptop?"

Carmen pointed to her satchel and since her place was so small he was able to reach it without getting completely out of bed.

"So, what exactly are we doing?"

"We are going to have a Superhero Movie Marathon," he said.

"According to Scarlett, that's like thirty movies!"

"Relax, doll, we're just going to give you a taste of a few fandoms," he said.

"Don't call me doll, and I would rather have a taste of you," she said and tried to distract Braxton with a trail of kisses along his neck.

"Carmen," he growled in warning but she kept going, letting her hand trail down his body to grab his cock.

Braxton grabbed her hand and brought it to rest on his chest.

"Come on, Brax. I need you," she said.

"You need to rest. I don't want to over-exert you, love."

She groaned and relaxed into him. "Fine, but let's make this a bit more interesting."

"Interesting how?"

"You don't want to over-exert me. One orgasm won't do that. So, what if I get one orgasm for every movie we watch. That's a built-in two-hour break," she offered.

Braxton laughed.

"This is how I know you have no clue about superhero movies. Movie first, then you get your orgasm."

CHAPTER 11

"**Y**ou want to tell me why you need to borrow my old riding jacket?" Baron said handing over the black leather jacket he used to wear daily.

"It's for the Wolverine costume I'm wearing to the Halloween party with Carmen."

Baron smirked and shook his head. "When Hunter told me you were getting serious with this girl I thought he was pulling my leg. Let me guess, she's going as Jean Grey."

Braxton shook his head.

"Nah, she's going as Storm," Braxton said.

"Storm was T'Challa's girl. Wouldn't that make more sense for a couple's costume?"

"It's not a couple's costume; we're going as friends."

"Look I'm definitely not the guy to give relationship advice but uh, don't you think you are taking this friends with benefits thing a little too far? You've spent the last month of weekends with this woman, and spend half your time during the week texting or daydreaming about her. Shouldn't you just drop the act and call her your girlfriend already?"

"She just got out of a relationship. Aren't you the one who told me it wasn't a good idea to be the rebound guy?"

"Again, you took my advice because?"

"I don't want to rush things and end up all broken over a woman, like you," Braxton said.

Baron flinched. "Fuck! Don't let what happened to me keep you from living your life. Learn from my mistakes but don't let them keep you from being happy." Baron stormed off before Braxton could apologize.

He would have gone after his brother but his Aunt Mirna suddenly appeared. She had a way of sneaking up on people when they least expected it and usually came with some cryptic message you would only figure out much later.

He smiled at his cooky aunt. "Hey, Mirna! To what do I owe this visit?"

She smiled and reached into her cloak. "Just wanted to make sure you got some of my berry jam."

She produced a jar of her legendary jam. It was made from a mixture of berries and edible flowers she foraged from the mountainside. Every year the family received a basket of jam-filled cookies and pastries to enjoy, but to receive an actual jar of the stuff was almost unheard of. Braxton would be a fool not to accept it.

"Thank you," he said taking it from her.

"Be sure you share some of that with your new lady friend. Maybe even use it tonight," Aunt Mirna said with a wink before skipping away back into the forest.

Braxton shook his head. Aunt Mirna really was a character, but he would take her advice on sharing it with Carmen. He knew she enjoyed to slather her morning toast with jam until it was more sugar than bread, and he couldn't wait to see the look on her face when she got a taste of Mirna's jam.

Carmen opened her door and swooned. Braxton had nailed his Wolverine costume and the sight of his bare chest and the way his carpet of chest hair trailed down into his jeans... She wanted to strip him completely naked and ride him until sunrise.

"You look amazing," Braxton said, breaking into her thoughts.

His gaze traveled over her skintight white catsuit and cape that Imena had helped her put together. Although the movies had shown Storm in a black catsuit, Carmen had fallen in love with the white and purple cape combo she'd found when researching the character online. She could see in his heated look that his thoughts had drifted to the same territory as hers.

She grabbed her bag and started to push him out the door. "I'd invite you in, but then I don't think we'd make the party."

Braxton blinked and then laughed. "You are absolutely right, love."

He followed her out and then helped her into his truck. She gave him directions to Yarrow's place and popped a couple of allergy pills when they were about thirty minutes out.

"What are those for?" Braxton asked.

"Yarrow is a dog groomer. The party will be mostly on the patio in his backyard, but it's better to be safe than sorry," Carmen said.

Braxton nodded. "You have an EpiPen? I can carry it for you just in case. That way you don't have to bring a bag inside."

"No, I never got around to getting one. Avoiding direct contact and taking over-the-counter allergy meds has been sufficient so far."

"Well, let me know if it stops working."

"Oh, I won't need to; you'll be able to tell. My skin gets all blotchy and I sneeze like a maniac."

"Noted. I'm guessing you won't be drinking tonight since it's probably not a good idea to mix allergy meds and alcohol."

"I'll have one drink, not because of the meds, but because I'm a total lightweight. Scarlett makes these crazy cocktails. Last year she made a poison apple martini and this year she's been raving about her latest creation, a candy corn cocktail."

"Candy corn is the worst Halloween candy," Braxton laughed.

"Exactly, but it's basically just sugar, so it can't be too bad in cocktail-form," Carmen said.

"Alright, what else typically happens at this party, other than drinking?"

"I'm not spoiling anything more. Besides we're almost there and you'll get to see for yourself."

Braxton pulled up to the black and white thatched roof cottage, with its white picket fence and red brick drive and turned to look at Scarlett.

"This is Yarrow's house? Not Amayah's?"

Carmen laughed. "I know, right. The interior is definitely more modern. He has a huge workshop in the back for his motorcycle but Yarrow has a thing for nostalgic buildings."

"Good to know."

They got out of his truck and walked around the side following the sounds of the Monster Mash and deep male laughter.

"Oh, you're here!" Amayah rushed toward them both, wearing in a little black dress and covered in green body paint.

Carmen and Amayah hugged and gushed over each other's costumes while Braxton tracked Yarrow Lupin as he made his way over to them. He was shirtless and wearing just a pair of torn khaki shorts. Also covered in green body paint. They were dressed as the Hulk and She-Hulk.

Braxton knew of Yarrow from their high school football days. Yarrow and the Sowell High Reapers had been the only team to beat Braxton and the Edgewood High Bears. Killing his undefeated streak and taking the championship year after year until Yarrow graduated. Braxton didn't hold any grudges against the man but it was hard not to puff out his chest a little as the man approached.

"Braxton Cross," Yarrow said holding out his hand.

Braxton smirked and took the man's hand squeezing hard.

"Yarrow Lupin, it's nice to see you."

They stood there a moment sizing each other up before Amayah nudged Yarrow in the side. "Now that Carmen is here, we can start the festivities," she said.

"Right, this way, Cross. Let the women do their thing. They'll come get us when they are ready," Yarrow started to walk away and Carmen gave Braxton a peck on the cheek before taking off with Amayah in the opposite direction.

Braxton shook his head before following Yarrow onto the massive wooden deck. The grill was going with massive steaks, manned by someone dressed as Hawkeye. Behind the bar Scarlett was dressed as Black Widow and handed off the bottle of vodka to another man dressed as The Winter Soldier.

"I guess by superhero party, you meant a Marvel Party," Braxton said.

Yarrow shrugged. "Nah, it just so happened that we all chose Marvel characters. Except, Imena, but she's dressed as RBG."

Braxton chuckled. "So, what do the men do while the women do their thing?"

"We drink beer and play darts or cards while the girls gossip and get tipsy."

"Is that what their thing is? Getting drunk and gossiping?"

"Pretty much. When they are drunk enough then the karaoke will start."

Braxton cringed. "Karaoke? You don't seem the type."

"I'm really not, but anything for my girl. You understand that, right?" Yarrow asked.

The look Yarrow shot him was more warning than anything else. Braxton didn't need a translator to get the hint. Yarrow was open to putting aside all the reasons they'd never even tried to be friendly before, to make Amayah happy. That also included kicking Braxton's ass if he did anything to hurt Carmen because that would also make Amayah unhappy.

"I do. Carmen's happiness is my priority too," Braxton said.

With that out of the way, the slight increase in tension between them dissipated and Yarrow clapped Braxton on the back.

"Nice Wolverine costume by the way," he said.

Carmen couldn't help but keep her eyes on Braxton and Yarrow on the deck. She and the girls were all huddled around the bonfire. Scarlett had brought a pitcher of her candy corn cocktail over and was already refilling everyone's glass, although Carmen had barely taken a sip of her first one. She could already feel the heavily liquored sugar bomb lowering her inhibitions.

"So much hair! You sure Braxton's family doesn't have any bears in their bloodline?" Imena whispered to Vega.

"I mean, it's not likely, but even if there is, it's not enough to make them one of us," Vega whispered back.

"Ladies! You really need to work on your whispering skills, and that's not only gross but mean," Amayah said.

Scarlett laughed. "Sorry, Carmen. We know he's your boo and all but you have to understand that the Cross family have mad colonizer history in the area. It's going to take us awhile to get used to being nice to one."

"Why? It didn't take long for Vega to get nice with Hunter," Carmen snapped.

"She's got you there," Artemis chuckled.

"That was different," Vega huffed.

"No, it's not. Anyway, you two look adorable together," Artemis said, which caused everyone to pause for a moment.

"Thank you, but we are just friends," Carmen said.

The whole group groaned.

"Now you sound like Savita," Vega said.

Savita raised her middle finger over the top of her phone without looking up.

"If you're just going to be on the phone all night, you could have stayed home. At least then you'd be able to get with the times and actually video chat your long distance not boyfriend," Imena said.

"Ugh, you and Arin make less sense than Carmen and Braxton pretending they aren't a couple."

"What's this about now?" Carmen asked.

"Arin is Savita's childhood bestie. Circumstances kept them from seeing each other for years and even though they have stayed in touch for whatever reason, they refuse to actually see each other. Not a single picture or video chat since they were like ten years old," Artemis filled in.

"I'm sure I can get a photo from Geon. He's Arin's cousin." Scarlett offered.

"Geon?"

"Chef Kim. Arin's family owns Sowell Garden and Flower Café."' Scarlett said.

"Oh, and when did it become Geon and not Chef Kim?" Amayah said.

Scarlett blushed and emptied her glass before changing the subject once again. "Are we drunk enough for karaoke yet?"

"I know I am," Carmen said.

"Not even close," Artemis said reaching for the pitcher of booze.

Imena and Vega both accepted more of the orange concoction, but Amayah and Savita also turned it down.

"I'm not singing tonight," Savita said.

"Oh, thank god. I love you like a sister, but my ears..." Vega said.

Savita flicked her off and buried herself into her phone once again.

"I'm tipsy enough," Amayah said and stood.

After the others downed their drinks, they all migrated over to the porch where Yarrow had just finished setting up the fancy karaoke stand he'd gotten Amayah the previous Christmas. Carmen went to stand by Braxton, but he pulled her into his lap.

"Brax," she hissed and tried to move away but he held her firm.

"Indulge me in this and I'll make it up to you later. I'm too tipsy to keep my hands off you right now," he whispered.

"How much did you drink?" she whispered back.

"This is only my second beer," he chuckled.

"I didn't take you for a lightweight the way you sucked down scotch at the hotel."

"I'm not, but it doesn't take much when it comes to you," he said, brushing his lips gently against the back of her neck.

Carmen's eyes fluttered closed and she nearly moaned as he flicked his tongue over a particularly sensitive spot. If they weren't in public, Carmen would have ground her hips against him, teasing him the same way he was teasing her, but they *were* in public. So, she gave his thigh a little pinch and focused on Amayah as she got ready to sing "I Put A Spell on You."

"Pay attention, this is going to be good," Carmen said.

Braxton rested his head on her shoulder, ending his teasing as Amayah began. She wasn't the best singer, but she put on a good show. Next Florian, Vega's brother did an off-key version of "Them Bones" by Alice in Chains, followed by Vega,

Scarlett and Imena wrecking "I'm in Love with a Monster" by Fifth Harmony.

Then it was Carmen's turn. For the first time in years, Carmen was nervous to sing. She had a good voice; she'd spent years as the lead soloist in her father's church. It was the one thing about her Noah had never tried to tear down. Yet, she hadn't sung in front of Braxton before and for whatever reason that made her feel jittery as she slid off his lap and went to take the mic from Vega.

She took a deep breath forcing her hands to stop shaking as the first notes of "Zombie" by the Cranberries began.

She was amazing. Braxton found himself leaning forward, totally wrapped up in Carmen as she belted out the classic Cranberries song. He had chills and he was hard as a rock in his pants. He'd known she'd had a set of pipes, their lovemaking had her hitting all kinds of high notes in bed, but this was something else. The general shyness Carmen had slid away as she really got into the song. Her eyes lit up and she went into mini rock star mode on the small stage Yarrow had set up.

If Braxton had had any doubt about his feelings for Carmen, they were long gone. Especially as she finished her song and her usual shy demeanor crept back in, she quickly bowed, handed off the microphone and scurried over to him. She flopped down into his lap a little frazzled and breathless, and he couldn't help himself. He shifted her legs to the side so he could kiss her properly.

"That was great," he said when he was finally able to pull himself from her sweet mouth.

"Thank you," she said and turned her attention back to the tiny stage where Calix Lupin was doing his best Michael Jackson impression while singing along to "Thriller."

Braxton didn't pay attention to any of it, nor to any of the other outlandish and downright awful performances of Carmen's friends. His attention was firmly on her, studying every smile, every grimace, every embarrassed laugh as she enjoyed the show.

"I know I'm supposed to be here to get to know your friends, but I really want to get you alone," Braxton whispered in her ear.

Carmen turned to look at him, heat in her eyes. "I've got one more song and then I'm all yours," she said and slid off his lap.

This time she sang "Haunted" by Beyoncé, and none of her friends offered any sort of protest when Braxton whisked her off towards the exit as soon as she was done.

"Drive safe," Amayah called after them.

Carmen turned to him then. "Maybe I should drive. I barely had two sips of alcohol and that was when we first arrived," she said.

Braxton felt okay to drive, but he had drunk more than he'd planned. While Calix had talked about his plans to reopen the old Sowell Gate Resort, they'd done a few shots between beers. So, he tossed Carmen his keys.

"Let's hit the road, love," he said before climbing into the passenger side.

Carmen got into the driver's seat and had to adjust it so it was comically close to the steering wheel.

"I can't believe you are letting me drive your truck," Carmen laughed.

"It's a first for sure, but I trust you," Braxton said and he meant it.

If he could trust her with his truck maybe he could work up the nerve to trust her with the truth of his feelings for her.

CHAPTER 12

Carmen smiled to herself as she snapped another shot of Braxton snoring away on her too tiny mattress. A mattress that was now on the floor after they broke the bedframe the previous night. He snorted and rolled over, pulling the covers over his face. Carmen sighed and set down her camera, before picking up her third slice of toast and jam.

She hoped Braxton didn't mind that she'd basically finished what was left of the heavenly mixed berry concoction he'd introduced her to last night. Of course, the first time she'd tasted it was by licking it from his large fingers and later lathing it off his flat nipples. He'd used half the jar on her body last night. It was only fitting she finish it off herself that morning.

She sat there munching away on her toast, just watching Braxton sleep. She'd never been so obsessed with a man before. From his monster feet to his monster cock, her eyes feasted on him like she feasted on her toast and jam. Only unlike her hunger for food, she just couldn't seem to get enough of Braxton. She shoved the last piece of her toast into her mouth and grabbed the almost empty jar of jam.

Maybe she just needed to satisfy her Braxton craving with a literal feast. As she tossed the covers away from him, his morning wood sprung free from the sheets and she licked her lips. How many times had Braxton woken her with his mouth on her vagina? She had no idea but she was about to return the favor. Dipping her finger into the jam jar she got the last little glob before smearing it over his cock with her hands.

He moaned, his hips shifting to meet her touch. She looked up expecting to see him looking back at her, but his eyes were still closed, even though his bottom lip was now tucked between his teeth. She licked her hand clean, not wanting to waste any of the jam before she turned her attention to Braxton's jam-covered cock.

"You just gonna admire it or are you going to clean up the mess you made," Braxton's raspy morning groan spurred her on. She licked her lips before licking him from base to tip, over and over until the only bit of jam left was right at the tip of him. Then she wrapped her lips around him and suckled until his hips bucked, trying to force himself deeper.

"Fuck, Carmen, you're killing me," he gasped.

She popped him out of her mouth and kissed her way up his stomach and chest.

"I'll finish you off with my mouth, once you tell me where I can buy more of that jam," she teased, stroking him with her hand.

"If there was such a place, you'd be the first to know. Sadly, the only way you'll get more is if I can manage to sneak a pastry or two to you over Christmas," he said.

"Damn, I guess you won't be able to finish until Christmas," she said and tried to roll off the bed.

Braxton grabbed her by the waist and rolled them both so that she was pinned under his massive body. His mouth captured hers and before she knew it, he'd slid on a condom then inside of her.

"I think I'll finish us both right now," he growled, rolling his hips.

Carmen matched his thrusts without shame. She'd only been teasing about not finishing him off. She wasn't that cruel, and this was definitely a preferable turn of events.

Carmen was taking more pictures of him.

After he'd finished them both this morning, he'd insisted on driving her to his workshop so he could replace her bed with one that wouldn't break when they got a little wild.

Of course, the moment they'd gotten to his workshop she'd had to pull out her camera and capture what she called "The aura of Braxton". She'd documented everything from him sketching out his idea, to him choosing the wood before gearing up to get started. Her bed wouldn't be done in just a day, but she'd insisted in capturing every aspect of the beginning stages.

So here he was working with wood while sporting massive wood in his pants. He might be in his element, but Carmen was a major distraction, with her bending herself into all sorts of positions to get the perfect shot of him and his work. She was so focused; she didn't seem to notice how turned on she was making him.

She finally let the camera fall from her face revealing a smile bigger than he'd ever seen from her.

"I think I could take a million pictures of you and never have enough," she said.

Braxton stopped what he was doing and smiled at her. "You can take all the pictures you want, love. In the bedroom, outside the bedroom. On one condition."

"And what is that?" Carmen asked.

"You take some of yourself, for me," he said.

"You'd want pictures of me? Nudes I bet," she laughed.

Braxton pulled her into his arms. "Of course I wouldn't turn down nudes but I'd love a picture of you when you're sleeping and peaceful, or one of you taking your first sip of coffee in the morning," he said.

Carmen made a face before picking her camera up and fussing with some settings before setting it down with the lens facing them. She pulled them back a few steps before wrapping her arms around him. "Smile," she said.

Braxton barely had time to react before the flash of her camera let him know that whatever timer she'd set had finished. She then went to the camera and looked at the results. A snort of laughter escaped her.

"Let's try that one more time. It's a ten-second timer this time; three shots will follow, in case you smile too late again," she said.

She jogged back over to him but Braxton had a better idea for a photo. He lifted her up wrapping her legs around him and pressed his forehead to hers before kissing her nose. His timing was perfect. The camera flashed three times.

Carmen shook her head before kissing him. He reluctantly set her down but kept on kissing her until she pulled away.

"Those probably came out terrible," she muttered before retreating to check her camera. This time however she brought it over for him to see as well.

The pictures hadn't turned out terrible. In fact, they'd come out better than Braxton had planned.

"I'd like copies of those please," he said.

Carmen looked like she would rather delete them, but instead, she nodded and turned her camera off.

"Mind showing me one of those trails you bragged about before I have to head back to Sowell?"

Braxton knew she was trying to put some distance between them and as much as he hated it, he didn't want to push and end up scaring her off for good, so he smiled and nodded.

"Sure can!" He put as much enthusiasm as he could muster in the statement, before leading her out of his workshop.

Carmen still wasn't ready to hear his truth, but now he had proof that she felt for him the same way he felt for her. The way she'd looked at him in those pictures was clear. She was in love with him. Anyone with half a brain could see that, but he would have to wait for her to realize it too. One thing was for sure, when she was ready, he would be ready. His four-step plan now included a fifth step. As Carmen got distracted with her camera again, Braxton pulled out his phone to call a fellow artisan to commission the ring he hoped to one day give to Carmen.

Braxton had not been lying about the view from his family's private trails. The gorgeous scenery was almost enough to distract Carmen from the way her heart raced after reviewing the photos of Braxton and her in his workshop. The way they looked at each other had rivaled some of the most in-love newlyweds Carmen had had the honor of shooting.

Carmen turned around to see Braxton lingering a little way behind her. He waved and flashed her a lopsided grin that had butterflies fluttering in her stomach.

Fuck. How could I have let this happen?

She was falling in love with Braxton Cross. The exact opposite of what she had planned. The good news was it wasn't too late to course-correct. They'd been hanging out for a little over a month. Maybe this should be their last visit for a while. She had her own place, her own business to keep afloat. She picked up her camera and took a few more shots before turning back to Braxton.

"I should get back before it gets too late," she said.

Braxton stopped in front of her, but didn't pull her into his arms. She could tell by the questioning look in his eyes that he knew she was pulling away. At least this time he didn't try to sway her, or call her out on her retreat.

"If that's what you want," he said.

"I do. I mean, I have some editing that needs to get done, and I'm sure you have some work you need to catch up on."

"Alright, give me a second to wrap up a few things and I'll take you back."

The smile on his face didn't reach his eyes and Carmen felt like complete shit. This was not how things were supposed to be between them. Yet, Carmen couldn't afford to let things go like they had been. She'd promised herself that she would get used to being on her own before she got with anyone new.

She sat on Braxton's front porch while she waited for him to do whatever he had needed to do. She could have waited inside but she felt it was emotionally safer for her to stay outside. If she got anywhere remotely private with Braxton the odds of her ending up under him grew exponentially.

After almost twenty minutes and no sign of Braxton, Carmen began to worry.

"Where are you?" she said to herself as she stretched her neck to look around.

Carmen could see the door to his workshop was cracked open, but no sign of Braxton. She got up from her spot on his porch and made her way over to the workshop. She could hear Braxton's voice as she got closer.

"You shouldn't be here. Who let you on site anyway?" Braxton asked.

"I have every right to be here; I'm still a Cross," a female voice said.

Carmen froze just outside the door.

"Not for much longer. You need to get out of here before you end up disappeared," Braxton hissed.

"Is that a threat, Brax? You going to disappear me like your father disappeared your aunt?"

"Again, I ask what are you doing here? Baron's cabin is on the other side of the compound."

"I didn't come to see Baron. I came to see you. I know you were pissed that I chose Baron over you back in the day. Maybe you and I can come to an agreement," the woman said.

"I was only pissed because we'd made a bet on whom you'd drop your panties for first. I lost a hundred bucks on that bet but turns out I was the winner after all. Now leave," Braxton said.

"Your family will never be rid of me. Not after what you all have done," the woman shrieked.

"You're one determined chick, you know that?"

"I'm glad you noticed. I am determined. I'll stop at nothing to get what I want," the woman said.

Carmen moved away from the door just in time to miss being hit by it as it swung open. A blonde woman in a fur coat and stilettos came striding out in a huff. She stopped upon seeing Carmen and eyed her up and down.

"Word of advice. Don't let yourself fall in love with any of these Cross bastards. You'll get nothing in return," the woman smirked before continuing on.

Carmen watched the woman go even as she heard the loud crash of something inside the workshop. Braxton came out a second later looking tired and pissed off.

"Where you standing there this whole time?"

Carmen studied Braxton for a moment. She had no idea what was up with that woman but there was one thing for sure. She would have to be careful with her heart around Braxton. Noah had hurt her for sure, but Braxton was quickly gaining the power to destroy her.

"You were gone for longer than I thought. I saw the door was open so I came to see what was taking you so long and that woman came out. Who is she?"

So much for playing it cool, Carmen.

She hadn't meant for that last question to come out as an accusation. It was clear from the discussion she overheard that Braxton didn't have an intimate relationship with the woman. The anger in Braxton's eyes softened and he pulled Carmen into a hug.

"That was my older brother's soon to be ex-wife. She's nothing but trouble and I can't wait for her to be out of my family's life for good," Braxton sighed.

"Oh," Carmen said.

She had no idea what else to say to that. She didn't want to pry into his family's personal business. Braxton pulled away and took her hand in his.

"I'll take you home now. I'm sorry for the delay."

He started to pull her toward his truck but Carmen dug in her heels.

"Braxton wait!"

He stopped and turned back to her. She shuffled her feet second-guessing her split-second decision. "I kind of want to get some sunset shots from the ridge. Do you mind if I stay a little longer?"

Braxton tilted his head to the side studying her for a moment before a slow smile crept across his face. "Of course, I don't mind. Although, what about all the editing you need to do?"

He was calling her bluff. Giving her a way out, and damn if that didn't make her want to stay more.

"There is always editing to do, but today is just so beautiful, and who knows when I'll get another chance to come out here," she said.

"You can come anytime you want, love. In fact," Braxton scooped her off the ground and into his arms, "I think I should make you come right now."

"I'd like that," Carmen whispered against his mouth.

CHAPTER 13

Carmen woke up to Braxton's mouth on her clit and his beard tickling her inner thighs. Her back arched off the bed as she reached down grabbing hold of his thick brown hair. In the last three months of weekends, she'd learned this was his favorite way to start their days together. It was hers too.

"Fuck, Brax!" she cried as she orgasmed.

He licked her clean before smiling up at her. "Morning, Carmen," he said before positioning his morning wood right at her entrance.

Her primed flesh accepted him with ease and she reached up gripping the headboard as he drove into her.

"Fuck, I thought we were hiking today!" she exclaimed.

"Snow hit early, trails are closed," he chuckled, before flipping her onto her stomach and entering her from behind.

She gripped his thick, hairy thighs to keep herself in the perfect angle for his deep thrusts to hit her right where she needed to go over the edge once more.

"Oh, the first snow! I've got to get pictures," she gasped.

"You want the first snow, I'll give it to you," he said just before pulling out. He tore off the condom and let himself go all over her back and thighs.

"You're sick, you know that?" Carmen giggled crawling off his massive bed.

Normally, they spent their time at her place in Sowell City, but this weekend he'd insisted on showing her the trails on his side of the mountain. So, she had come to him. The drive to Edgewood wasn't as bad as she thought it would be. It had taken a little longer than expected, as she'd stopped several times to take a few shots along the way, but once she made it to the Cross Estate Braxton had whisked her to his cabin in the woods and gave her the erotic tour of his abode. She probably would have been too sore for the hike this morning anyway with how thorough he'd been last night.

Braxton followed her into the bathroom with a big grin on his face.

"I can't help it when you offer such inspiration for fantasies I never knew I had," he growled.

"Don't start. I'm serious about getting pictures of the first snow, even if we can't go up the trails right now," she said climbing into his massive shower.

She stood back while the water warmed up to her desired temperature, before stepping under the spray. Braxton disappeared into the water closet before joining her a few minutes later, his massive hands kneading the tension out of her body along with the heat of the spray.

"We'll go outside, see the snow, make a snowman or a fuck angel," he said.

"A what?"

"A fuck angel, you know, a snow angel but me fucking you while you're all spread out in the pristine snow," he said.

"You're silly," she laughed and finished rinsing off before getting out of the shower to find her clothes.

She'd brought an overnight bag but couldn't find it any-where.

"Check the closet," he said when she finally asked him what he did with her things.

Carmen shook her head when she entered the massive cedar lined walk in. Braxton may seem like a low maintenance mountain man, but boy did he have an extensive wardrobe. She wasn't sure she was even in a closet and not a pop-up REI Brooks Brothers mash-up. She had no idea where to even begin looking for her things, until she noticed a red bow tied to the bar of a mostly empty section of the closet. Mostly empty because he'd hung a few of her clothes up already.

She blinked a few times before she felt him wrap his arms around her waist. He was still dripping wet from the shower but she was also still naked so she didn't mind too much.

"What is this?" she asked.

"Happy three-month anniversary, love," he said and kissed her cheek.

Carmen turned to face him and shook her head. "I didn't realize we were a couple let alone sharing-closet-space offi-cially," she said.

She felt Braxton tense at her words, his smile falling from his face. "Carmen, we've spent every weekend together since we met. I started calling you love a month after that. How did you not know we were a couple?"

She bit her lip; it was silly actually now that she thought about it. As much as she'd fought the idea of being more than casual with Braxton, nothing between them had ever been casual. Not from the beginning and certainly not now.

"Right, but can we say two months? I'm more comfortable with that," she said.

Braxton shook his head and lifted her onto the clothes island.

"Fuck no, Carmen. You were mine from the moment I laid eyes on your cosplaying ass in that hotel," he said shoving himself into her.

Braxton reached between their bodies using the pad of his thumb to press firmly against her clit as he pounded into her. She fisted her hands in his chest hair and pulled him in for a kiss. They both orgasmed so intensely that their joint cries echoed off the walls around them.

"Fuck," Carmen hissed as she felt him filling her with his seed.

"Exactly, Carmen. You're mine and there's no question about that," he said, still holding her tight.

"Yeah, yeah but Brax, you didn't use a condom," Carmen gasped.

She wanted to sound calmer but inside she was panicking. It was just one time; it should be fine.

"Carmen, is there something you need to tell me?" Braxton asked pinning her with a serious look as she had a mild panic attack.

"I'm not on birth control. I mean I am, but it's not effective yet. There was an issue with my last prescription and I missed the recall notice because it was sent to Noah's and ...." She took a deep breath before continuing to ramble. "I'm sorry. I should have told you. I should have been more careful. I mean nothing is one hundred percent and..."

Braxton cut her off with a kiss. "It's okay. I mean, it's not okay that you didn't tell me about the birth control, but it's not the end of the world, alright? Honestly, I'm not a fucking magician, there were times I let myself get real close before I put a condom on. Neither of us are saints and we both know I got zero patience when I'm ready to get in you," he said.

"Wait what! This isn't the first time?"

"Come on sweetheart, you don't remember those weekends when you'd climb on top in the middle of the night? I never finished inside you without a condom but I've definitely been in you. I wouldn't have let it happen if I knew you were off the pill."

"No!" Carmen felt like crying as she took a real deep dive into their encounters. There had been times when she'd woken up horny as fuck and half asleep just to fuck and not exactly caring about anything but her pending orgasm.

"Shhh, it's okay. We'll get dressed and go into town for a visit to the pharmacy. If it's too late and you're already pregnant from past oversight it's not ideal timing but I'm good with it."

Carmen's eyes bugged. "You're good with it. You. Braxton Cross. Are good with it?"

"Are you not?"

"No! I mean, sure I thought about having kids one day, just not like this and not with," she stopped herself from saying you but it was already there hanging between them.

Braxton took a step back from her and ran his hand over his face. The tears she'd been holding back started to fall as she slid off the table.

"I don't mean it like that. I've told you how I was raised, strict religious parents who disowned me when they found birth control in my room. I was still a virgin at the time but they didn't believe me and were appalled that I'd do anything to prevent one of 'God's miracles'. Having a baby out of wedlock? That's not something I ever dreamed of and I'm just wrapping my head around the concept of us being a real couple. So no, I never imagined us having a child because we were taking this a week at a time and we're good together. So very, very good together but you can't say you've thought about it either. You really can't. You haven't, have you? I mean, you're obviously ahead of me in all of this..."

Carmen was a rambling mess. Words just kept spilling out of her mouth as she tried to explain, with Braxton staring stone-faced at her. What finally got her mouth to stop moving was Braxton reaching around her to get into one of the drawers hidden in the table he'd just fucked her on, retrieving an ornately carved jewelry box.

"To answer your question, yeah, I have thought about us in the forever kind of way. Did I plan on doing this now? Fuck no, but I believe in laying all the cards on the table before any major decisions are made. So, here it is. Carmen Elise Quinn, I am completely and utterly gone over you. This isn't a proposal; I know it would be a mistake to do so now. Just know that I made this box to house the ring of my future wife. I had a friend of mine custom make a wedding set and everything. I'm not going to show it to you but I'm telling you it's in there for when we are ready. Not if, but when, Carmen. That's how serious I am about you. I get that it's too soon for you, you need more time, this is definitely not ideal circumstances but this is my truth where we are concerned."

The box itself was beautiful and she knew whatever it held would be equally so. Her fingers itched to touch it but she held back.

"I don't expect you to marry me if I am pregnant or get pregnant," she said instead.

"I'm trying to tell you, Carmen, that baby or not, I'd happily make you legally mine right now if I could. I didn't start calling you love for shits and giggles. I love you and I want to be with you. If I wasn't sure of that, I never would have allowed myself to finish inside of you. I'm a magician with a condom remember? Had a whole stash right at my fingertips and didn't touch them because I am a possessive asshole and couldn't help staking my claim."

"I... Brax," Carmen began but he put his finger to her lips stopping her.

"Get dressed, we'll go to the pharmacy. I think that's the most important thing for us to do right now, right?"

Carmen nodded and turned towards her clothes. She could hear Braxton tucking away the jewelry box before shrugging into his own clothes. It wasn't until they emerged from the bathroom that they noticed how much snow had fallen while they were otherwise occupied.

"Well, if this ain't a sign from the man on high himself," Braxton said with a whistle.

Looking out the wide front windows, Carmen could see that there wasn't just a couple of inches of snow on the ground, but several feet and it was still falling. They were higher up on the mountain than the town below, but Carmen knew there was too much for them to even get down there, let alone for the store to actually be open.

"This is the first snow; it shouldn't be too bad right? Might even clear up by this afternoon?" Carmen did her best to remain hopeful.

Braxton went into the kitchen and dug out his emergency radio before switching it on. The first thing they heard was news of an out of season blizzard. "You're lucky I'd already planned for us to be locked in the cabin this weekend, otherwise we'd have to make the trek to the main house," Braxton said shrugging into his jacket.

"What are you doing? You can't go out there," Carmen said.

"Yeah, I can. Especially if you want to be warm and toasty and safe by the fire tonight. Sowell City doesn't get snow like we do, and a blizzard isn't nothing to play about. So, sit tight and let me make sure we can safely hold out here for the next few days," he said before leaving out the front door.

Carmen watched from the window as Braxton went to his workshop across the way, emerging with a sled full of stuff she couldn't see because it was covered by a tarp. She hadn't wanted to fight with him, hated the hurt she'd seen in his eyes. They were just in an impossible situation. Their agreement to be no more than fuck buddies had obviously been their first mistake, and now Carmen also had to worry about an unplanned pregnancy. She'd do just about anything to erase the last thirty minutes if it meant she and Braxton could go back to the crazy in lust fling they'd had.

She moved over to the massive fireplace in front of the couch, ignoring the framed photograph of her and Braxton from her first visit to the mountain. It was the weekend she'd realized she was falling for Braxton. The chemistry between them radiated from the photograph like rays of the sun, warming her heart and nearly chasing away the guilt she felt for being so harsh with Braxton earlier. Carmen started to load the fireplace with wood. Anything to keep her hands busy and at least *try* to keep her mind off of Braxton and his declaration of love. Well. Not that exactly. She'd known for a while now that Braxton loved her and the part that killed her was that she loved him too. But there was no denying that Carmen just wasn't ready for a commitment, especially not one that involved babies and wedding bells.

Ding. Dong. Ding. Dong. The chiming ringtone of her phone broke into her thoughts. She stopped tossing wood into the massive fireplace and went to retrieve her phone. Not surprisingly, the group chat with her friends was super active.

I: It's the first snow!

S: I'm not a fan.

A: Carmen are you still in Edgewood? I heard there is a blizzard warning for that side of the mountain.

Carmen smirked and texted back.

C: Warning? No it's a full blizzard. I'm stuck until it clears.

S: That's not the attitude of a woman who gets to be snowed in with her beast of a lover.

A: Did something happen? You need us to rescue you?

C: It's fine. We had a bit of a disagreement this morning but nothing serious.

I: This is a turning point for your relationship. Trust your gut.

A: Now isn't the time for cryptic messages Imena. Carmen, Yarrow says we can get someone out to you in an hour if need be.

C: I'm fine I promise. We just need to have another discussion about what our relationship is.

S: Seriously! You're still denying that you two are mad for each other?

C: No! That's the problem. He made space for me in his closet and he got me a ring!

A: Oh my god! He proposed! Tell me you said yes!

S: Obviously she didn't otherwise this would be a different conversation entirely.

C: He didn't propose. Hell, I don't even know what the ring looks like. I just know he has one. It's complicated.

I: Like I said. Trust your gut.

S: Look, Carmen, I know you think you need more time before getting into another relationship but girl, it's been three months of the you and Braxton show. I suggest you take a real good look at why you are so hesitant, and if it has anything to do with what other people will think.

A: I know I'm usually the more practical one, but I agree with Scarlett and Imena. Take it from someone who tried to deny her true feelings for the man she loves. The sooner you stop overthinking things and let yourself love and be loved, the better. You'll kick yourself for spending so much time denying what you two have.

Carmen lit the kindling under the giant pile of wood she'd managed to shove into the fireplace. She watched the flames build as the wood caught. Soon there was a massive inferno and Carmen moved backwards hurriedly, afraid she'd maybe put too much in.

C: I'll keep you guys posted.

She tucked her phone into her pocket and turned to the front window. The snow was falling heavier now and she could only barely catch glimpses of Braxton trudging around in his coat outside. The fire in the fireplace was throwing off major heat and Carmen was glad she'd thought about starting it, now that she saw just how bad it was outside. The heat would be welcoming to Braxton when he came inside. He'd also probably be hungry. Neither of them had eaten before the storm had hit and he'd rushed out to get the cabin prepared for them to be comfortable.

Moving to the kitchen, Carmen got to work on breakfast and her apology. If they were going to be stuck inside for a few days, she'd need to come up with a good one, so that things weren't as awkward between them. An apology that would start with her admitting she was in love with him too. Carmen may not be ready for what Braxton was offering, but it was unfair to both of them to deny the obvious.

Braxton was happy to have something to do outside of the cabin; the cold temperatures and manual labor kept him from dwelling on the shitstorm of his apparently new relationship with Carmen. He'd just finished topping off the backup generator for the cabin when he saw the lights of Hunter's snowmobile approaching.

"Braxton, you asshole! Ma's been trying to reach you all morning," Hunter yelled.

"Keep your voice down! I got company," Braxton hissed as his cousin pulled to a stop in front of him.

Hunter smirked and revved his engine. "Think your girlfriend heard that? You planning to keep Carmen locked away here the whole blizzard. You know damn well Ma ain't gonna stand for that. You know how she gets, wants us all in the big house to weather out the storm together," Hunter said.

"Yeah, well, it's not a good time for her to be introduced to the whole clan, okay?" Braxton said.

"Trouble in paradise?"

Braxton snorted. "Just tell mom I'm good out here. Storm shouldn't be too bad."

"Alright man, but it's your funeral. Even Bechet and Isis are moving into his old room for this one," Hunter said.

Braxton frowned. "I didn't know they were here?"

"Maybe if you would have been listening at dinner this week, instead of plotting your weekend rendezvous, you would have known that they were. An apology visit, since Isis's family claimed the first Christmas with the newlyweds."

"Yeah, definitely not going," Braxton said.

"Well, you know to reach out if you need anything."

Hunter took off, hitting Braxton with a spray of snow in his wake. Braxton brushed it off. There wasn't much else he could do outside, especially with how heavy the snow was falling now. So, he made his way back inside fully expecting it to feel like doom and gloom. Instead, he found that not only had Carmen started a fire in the fireplace, but she was dancing to the radio as she plated his favorite breakfast; pancakes, sausage and eggs.

The domesticity of it should have been a wet blanket, given the circumstances, but instead warmth bloomed in his chest. Fuck, she looked good in this role. In this place; his home, in his kitchen, cooking for him. He kicked off his boots and shrugged out of his coat before pulling her into his arms and kissing her.

"How dare you?" he growled.

Carmen made a face before smacking him with the wooden spatula. "What do you mean how dare I? Dare I what? Not make you breakfast as a peace offering?"

"Give me a glimpse at the future you are insistent on denying us," he replied.

Carmen groaned and set the spatula down. "I never said it was impossible. All I said was I'm not there yet," she said.

"Well, I've got at least the next two to three days to get you there," he said.

"Fine, as long as you promise to wear condoms from now on," she grumbled.

"No, cuz if my original plan doesn't work for whatever reason, I am most definitely trapping your ass with my offspring," he said and picked up the plates she had served and moved them over to the small kitchen table by the window.

"Guess you're going to be easing the tension with your hand then, because this is off limits for uncovered dicks," she said, gesturing at her vagina before sitting down across from him.

"Alright, guess we'll be seeing if your tight little ass can take more than one of my fingers tonight," he said before taking a bite of his pancakes.

Carmen inhaled sharply and he saw the slap coming, grabbing her hand before it made contact with his face, he licked the palm of her hand in the pattern she enjoyed when he did the same on her pussy.

"Braxton!"

"That's good practice, but I'm sure we can work on that sweet upper register of yours after we fuel up. Maybe warm you up some more with my tongue before I give it to you good," he smirked.

Carmen looked outraged, but the way she squirmed in her chair let him know she was well on her way with being on board with his plans.

Braxton thought he'd had the upper hand but Carmen put her foot down about the condom issue. They'd ended up back in bed after breakfast without much of a conversation, and without Carmen giving her apologetic speech to him. As much as Braxton was playing their fight off as nothing, there had been a marked difference in their love-making. For the first time since they'd started things, it had really just been sex. Amazing sex, but sex that left her feeling hollow inside.

Carmen sat up in bed, clutching the sheets to her chest. Panic swelled inside of her. She didn't want to lose Braxton. Didn't want to lose what they had, especially not like this. Tears began to well in her eyes and she climbed out of bed. She didn't want to wake him up with her sobbing. She needed to pull herself together before she could talk to him about this.

The hot spray of Braxton's massive shower did its best to relax the tension in her muscles, but despite it all, she stood under the water clutching her body and shaking as she cried. At this point, Carmen realized it wasn't just about Braxton but about herself. How she'd been lying to herself this whole time. How she'd been blocking her own happiness more than Noah and her parents ever had.

I will no longer be my own barrier.

Carmen repeated the thought over and over until she calmed down enough to stop crying. The water had already run itself cold a long time ago and now the icy bite brought her out of her internal dialogue and back to the present. She stepped out of the shower and made her way to Braxton's massive closet, where her clothes were still tucked away in her bag. With a new resolve, she slowly pulled out her things and hung them up in the space Braxton had made for her.

I will no longer be my own barrier.

Her new mantra settled over her like a heated blanket, providing a sense of comfort and a new resolve. She stepped back taking a moment to look at her clothes in his space, to see if the panic rose up again or if things still didn't feel right. No panic, no icky feeling came. It was just clothes in a closet. Carmen released the breath she hadn't known she was holding.

"I see you've unpacked," Braxton said from the door.

Carmen turned to find him smiling at her.

"I figured actions would work better than words to end our fight," Carmen said.

"Fight? What fight?" Braxton asked.

"Don't pretend like it didn't happen. It did, and it's important that we actually work through it, instead of ignoring or fucking it away," Carmen said.

Braxton sighed and closed the distance between them, his big strong arms wrapping around her and holding her close. "I jumped the gun and I'm not sorry about it."

"You did, I mean, not really. I should have been more honest with you about everything. I love you Braxton. I was afraid to say it earlier because I didn't want to make things complicated."

"Complicated?" Braxton snorted. "Love, the only complicated thing about us is the way we met. Everything else is as simple as those Gen Ursa Novels you devour. Two consenting adults who turned a complicated situation into a love for the ages."

"I'm going to ignore that slight against my reading choices, but other than that, Braxton Cross, you have just firmly cemented your romance hero status in my book."

Braxton shook his head. "The only way that works is if I got down on one knee right here and proposed."

"Oh god, please don't. I mean, I love you, but I was serious when I said I'm not ready for that level of commitment."

"I know, which is why I'm not going to, right now."

"Why do I feel like that 'right now' means I'll have to be on the lookout sometime in the next day or so?" Carmen asked.

"Because I want you in my life forever, and you know how impatient I can be when it comes to you," Braxton said.

"Well, be more patient."

"Aren't you at least curious about the ring?"

Carmen bit her lip. She was curious but she knew a trap when Braxton was setting one.

"Let me guess, if I say yes you'll show it to me and then I'll have to say yes because it will be that gorgeous and heartfelt," Carmen said.

"A man can hope," Braxton laughed.

"Fine, show me the ring."

Braxton let Carmen go to move around the center island. He pulled the ring box out of its hiding spot and set it out facing her.

"Before you open the box, I just need to say one thing," Braxton said.

Carmen put her hands on her hips and smiled sweetly at Braxton. "If you propose right now, I'm going to say no, just on principle."

"It's not a proposal, but Carmen, I was serious about this ring being something from my heart for my future wife. Opening that box will bare my entire soul to you. Something neither of us can take back. So, it's your choice. If you open it and can walk away without it stirring something deep inside of you, maybe your hesitation about us being together means more than you think. I'll be outside," Braxton said before leaving her alone with the box.

Carmen suddenly felt stupid for even asking about the ring. She stared at the box for ages. The curiosity at seeing what Braxton was talking about warred with her own fears about rushing things with him. Braxton hadn't proposed per say but there was no denying the weight of his words. She could not open the box at all, and it wouldn't mean the end of them together. The real issue was if she opened it. If she opened it and didn't like what she saw, or was indifferent to the obvious care and commitment he'd poured into it, that would surely be the end of things.

Then there was the third option and that was arguably the scariest for Carmen. So, she pushed the box away from her. She didn't want to give up Braxton or what they had just because she wasn't ready to commit. Carmen was almost to the door when she turned around and rushed back.

Fuck it! Just rip off the Band-Aid. If it's meant to be, then why fight it? I will no longer be a barrier to my happiness.

Ten minutes had passed, and Carmen was still in the closet. Braxton's heart raced so fast he swore it would hop out his chest and run laps around the bedroom like a Nascar driver. His pacing wasn't helping either. He'd been able to remain calm for about half a second after leaving Carmen alone with the ring he'd had custom made for her. He hadn't told her that, because she was already jumpy about committing.

His fear had turned into guilt. It was shitty of him to press the issue. There was only one outcome that would satisfy him and she'd already told him repeatedly that wasn't what she wanted right now. Braxton ran his hands through his hair and worked his jaw. Ten minutes was too long, she was either conflicted about opening the box or had already opened it and was too afraid to face him now that she knew she didn't actually love him enough to be with him. To make matters worse, no matter the outcome they were stuck together for at least the next twenty-four hours.

Stupid. Impatient. Asshole of the Year.

Braxton was just about to head to the guest room to get it ready for her when he heard her gasp. He froze in place. She'd opened the box. He was sure of it now. Turning around he headed for the closet. Carmen met him at the door and jumped into his arms.

"You are an impatient asshole and I should kick your ass right now but all I can say is yes! Braxton Cross, I've seen your soul and I want all parts of it."

She was crying and Braxton realized so was he.

Two Years Later

C armen snuggled with Braxton and their one-year-old son Brayden on the couch as snow drifted to the ground outside. Another early blizzard if you could believe it. Carmen smiled to herself thinking of just how much had changed in the last two years. Getting married, having Brayden, expanding her business. All things that two years ago seemed impossible. Now she couldn't imagine her life any different. Well, she could imagine today going differently. If Braxton hadn't kept her in bed late this morning, they would have already been at their house in Sowell instead of stuck at the cabin.

"I told you we should have headed to our place in Sowell yesterday. I'm going to have to cancel my portrait sessions on Monday," she grumbled.

"Probably the whole week, and you know damn well my mother was not letting us hit the road with Brayden with an impending storm. You're lucky she let us stay here in the cabin and not at the main house," Braxton replied.

"Please tell me we are at least well-stocked. I can't do another Cross family sleepover," Carmen said.

"What? We do them all the time, Mrs. Cross."

"You know what I mean."

"I do, and yeah, I made sure after the first time to have more than just three days on hand."

"Condoms too?"

"Now that may be a stretch," Braxton trailed kisses along her neck, his hands sliding under her sweater to caress her stomach. "I think it's time for Brayden's nap."

Upon hearing the word 'nap' Brayden screamed in protest. Carmen moved Braxton's hand away from her body and placed Brayden on the floor with a few of his toys as a distraction.

"His nap time isn't for another hour. Don't you have things to do before the storm gets bad?"

Braxton flopped over on the couch with a groan. "Woman, you're killing me. The only thing I want to do involves you on your knees and my dick in your sweet pussy."

"Ugh, I knew I should have gotten that damn IUD. We just got Brayden sleeping through the night in his own bed, and you really want to risk another one?"

"Carmen, you know I'd risk anything for you," he said.

"Too much if you ask me," she laughed allowing Braxton to pull her back into his embrace.

"Never too much," he replied.

Braxton was giving Carmen the eyes and she was about to give in when there was a knock on the front door. Braxton groaned before getting up to get it. There was no way it was good news if the family was bothering them with a blizzard outside. Carmen relaxed with Brayden but watched out the window to see Hunter speaking animatedly to Braxton.

"What's going on?" Carmen asked as Braxton started to grab his heavy coat and a flashlight.

"Baron hasn't made it off the mountain yet, and Hunter can't reach him on the radio," Braxton said.

STELLA WILLIAMS

Stella Williams is a Blogger and USA TODAY Bestselling Paranormal Romance & Urban Fantasy Author, who lives in Washington State. She has a degree in Anthropology from The University of California, Santa Cruz. Stella prides herself in using her studies to create diverse worlds and characters for her novels. You can find more about Stella Williams on her website: www.stellawilliamsauthor.com

ALSO BY STELLA WILLIAMS

Sowell Gate Universe
Wild Cross Family

Felling Bechet

Yarding Braxton

Branding Baron

Reclaiming Hunter
Monsters & Mayhem

Peak
Unforgettable Contemporary

Unforgettable Valentine

Maura's Men Universe
Bloodlines

His Soul To Keep

To Catch Akellah
Secret of Ceres

Ferocious

Dauntless

Earnest

Zenith
Langsmith Shifters

Coy Wolf

A Night Divine

Bird of Prey
Maura's Men

Xander's Claim

Claude's Conquest

Shane's Redemption

www.ingramcontent.com/pod-product-compliance
Lightning Source LLC
Chambersburg PA
CBHW030638190726
48286CB00008B/2565